OPERATION
WOLF
PACK

a Poppy McVie adventure

Titles by Kimberli A. Bindschatel

The Poppy McVie Series
Operation Tropical Affair
Operation Orca Rescue
Operation Grizzly Camp
Operation Turtle Ransom
Operation Arctic Deception
Operation Dolphin Spirit
Operation Wolf Pack

The Fallen Shadows Trilogy
The Path to the Sun (Book One)

OPERATION
WOLF
PACK

KIMBERLI A. BINDSCHATEL

Turning Leaf Books · Traverse City, MI

Published by Turning Leaf Productions, LLC.
Traverse City, Michigan

www.PoppyMcVie.com
www.KimberliBindschatel.com

Print ISBN-13:9780960026111

This is a work of fiction. Names, characters, businesses, places, events and incidents are either the products of the author's imagination or used in a fictitious manner. Any resemblance to actual persons, living or dead, or actual events is purely coincidental.

Thank you for purchasing this book and supporting an indie author.

For Smitty,
He understood my passion for animals and loved me
for it. I miss him.

With special thanks to the brave men and women of the U.S.F.W.S. and their counterparts around the globe who dedicate their lives to save animals from harm. Their courage and commitment is nothing short of inspiring.

May their efforts not be in vain.

The greatest thrill is not to kill but to let live.

~James Oliver Curwood, *The Grizzly King*

OPERATION
WOLF
PACK

CHAPTER 1

No way. I blinked, trying to clear my eyes. *Couldn't be.* No one could be that stupid. Could they?

I pulled over to the side of the road, flipped on the hazard lights, and got out.

"Hey! Hey there!" I yelled, waving my arms frantically. "Get back!"

The man glanced my way, a look of confusion on his face. He was standing ten feet from a full-grown, 1200-pound adult bison, with a squirming toddler in his arms.

"We just want a picture," he said to me, matter-of-fact, and continued another step, lifting his towheaded daughter as if he were going to set her on the bison's back.

"Step away right now! That's a wild animal. And a dangerous one." I took another cautious step toward them, careful not to startle the bison who was chewing a mouthful of prairie grass. Several yards away from the bison was a young calf.

Father-of-the-year looked at the bison, then back at me. "Seems friendly enough to me."

The bison paused her munching and fixed her eye on the man.

"Trust me, she's not. Now step back."

His wife lowered her phone and shrugged. "Come on, Al, bring Evie back on over here." At least she had some sense.

The bison stomped her foot, kicking up dust, and dropped

her head.

"Get back now!" I said, hurrying the man along.

With a snort, the bison stomped again, pawing at the ground. A warning.

A look of disappointment crossed the man's face as he reluctantly moved away from the animal. "Fine," he muttered.

"She feels threatened. Can't you see? She's about to charge."

The man turned away from the animal and slowly walked back toward his wife.

The bison stomped again, and rushed him.

"Run!" his wife screamed.

The man's expression changed to surprise as he spun to see the bison charging at him. He sprinted toward my car and managed to get behind it. The bison backed off.

The man started laughing. Laughing!

I was fuming. I stomped toward him. "Haven't you seen the signs? The park rules? Do *not* approach the wildlife."

He gave me a half shrug. "Yeah, but it ain't a bear."

Why is it that people are terrified of predators, but they see a herd of grazing bison and think it's a petting zoo? Apparently, this had become a problem in recent years, people getting too close for selfies. I didn't want to believe it.

I drew in a breath to check my temper before responding, "Believe me, an angry bison can be just as dangerous as a bear. Or even more so. Bison have injured more people here in Yellowstone than any other animal."

He gave me a look full of contempt and skepticism. "And just who are you?"

"I used to be a park ranger here." It was mostly true. I'd been a summer intern.

"Oh," he said, disappointed he may have to actually listen to me.

I shook my head. This guy needed a reality check.

"Approaching wildlife like that could get you kicked out of the park and possibly fined. Or worse, that bison could have gored you."

His eyes darted from me to the bison and back, then his expression turned back to disbelief. "No way."

"Do you know what an animal that size could do to your baby girl?"

He looked at his daughter as if seeing her for the first time as his child and not a prop for a picture. "Oh, maybe, I guess. I think we woulda been just fine though."

Exasperated, I rolled my eyes. "Please, just get back in your car and stay at least one hundred yards from any animal. *Any* animal."

He frowned, but set his daughter down on the ground, took her by the hand and led her to their car with his head held high and his chest puffed out. He had listened to me but he wasn't particularly happy about it.

His wife gave him a shrug of disappointment and followed him with her head down.

"Have a nice day," I said with a falsely cheerful wave, the old training kicking in.

I looked back at the bison. She raised her head and stuck out her tongue to wipe grass from her lip as she eyed me for a moment, as if to say, *thanks for getting rid of that pest.*

I grinned back at her. "You're welcome."

I'd stopped here at Ice Box Canyon, one of my favorite pullout spots on the northeast side of Yellowstone. Once the family sped away, I had the place to myself. I sat down on the edge of the wooden walkway along Soda Butte Creek. It flowed faster with the added runoff of spring. I listened to it gush and gurgle for a minute, drawing in several breaths of the fresh, clean air. I'd missed it here.

The high-pitched chitter of prairie dogs caught my attention. Two adults popped up onto the boardwalk and sat up on their haunches, singing away. They watched me with their big, round, black eyes, twitching at every movement that caught their attention. They were so cute.

If only I could spend a couple weeks here, watch the park bloom with the changing of the season, with all the new offspring, out testing their legs and wings. But I had to get to work.

I got back into my car and continued on, further into the park.

A few days earlier, I'd received a call from my boss to head to Idaho to investigate a wolf-related issue. Since I was in Montana at the time, I thought I'd make a side trip through Yellowstone. I wanted to talk to an old friend about the wolves and maybe dig up some memories of my summer here during my college days.

I followed the familiar road. Even though it had been— what?— six years, the place hadn't changed a bit, a testament to tireless conservation efforts and solid public policy.

The bright greens of spring made the valley seem to come alive. The rolling hills, dotted with occasional evergreens, spread before the backdrop of rocky peaks, the tips white with snow. This was a pristine landscape, a wilderness still in its prime.

I slowed for a small herd of pronghorn antelope to cross the road. They ran down a dip toward the river's edge and kicked up a gaggle of Canada geese. I rolled the window down to hear the geese honk as they lifted off.

A few more miles down the road, my phone rang. I pulled over to the side to take the call.

It was Greg, an analyst and tech support staff for my team. We worked well together, kinda like a brother-sister team where he was the annoying little brother.

"Yo," I answered.

"Yo to you. Where are you?"

"Yellowstone National Park. But you knew that. It's like you've got me chipped."

"That's not exactly—"

"What you don't know, is that I just had to save some idiot from winning a Darwin Award. I'm telling you, he was moments from a grisly death."

"Grizzly? You saw a bear?"

"No. Grisly, not grizzly. I saw a moron trying to set his little girl on the back of a bison to get a selfie. They both could have been trampled to death."

"No way."

"That's what I said."

"Seriously?"

"I just don't get it, Greg. People aren't afraid of bison and moose, but wolves and bears are— "

"Wolves are scary. They have big teeth."

"Bison have big hooves. And horns."

"Yeah, but they don't hide in your grandma's clothing and pretend to like you."

"Um. Okay." I had to think about that for a moment. *Nope. I got nothing.* "You got details about my case for me?"

"Yep." I heard the click-click-click of his keyboard. "Hyland wants you to investigate a guy named Jack Wade. He's a USDA-APHIS Wildlife Services agent and—"

"Wait. I'm investigating a federal agent? Isn't that the purview of—"

"Yes, but Hyland wants her own info on what's going on out there. You're to quietly poke around, undercover. There's been a rash of claims of livestock depredation by wolves in a concentrated area. I'm guessing maybe someone somewhere is thinking we might have a crooked agent who's taking bribes or something."

"I don't understand. What does one have to do with the other?"

"Idaho compensates ranchers for missing livestock, but recently, they changed the rules. They no longer cut checks unless they're government-confirmed losses, government being a USDA-APHIS Wildlife Services agent. Enter Jack

Wade. When a claim is filed, he performs an inspection and determines if the loss was due to wolf depredation. And since there have been so many lately, well, they think something may be fishy."

"Gotcha."

"She says you're to run point, and—"

"Me? Run point? As in it's my op?" She'd told me, but I still couldn't believe it.

"Yeah, that's what run point means."

"Right." *My own op. Wow.* Sure, I was a good agent and had an exceptional arrest record, one I was proud of, but of my list of credentials, managing a team wasn't exactly my forte. I was more of a loner.

"You're to decide how best to integrate Tom and Mike. And Dalton when he gets back."

Dalton. Where had he gone? Dalton was my partner and just as we were working out the details about what to do about our attraction to each other, he'd disappeared. "Yeah, right. Dalton. Have you heard from him?" I said, trying not to sound too desperate to know.

"Nope. He's on vacation, remember?"

"Oh yeah. Right. So, Hyland said for me to run point, huh?"

"Yep. I've got her scheduled to check for a head injury."

"Very funny." Maybe I was the only choice, with Dalton being gone, and Mike under discipline from that stunt he'd pulled in Chicago. But there was still Tom.

Hyland always had a reason, regardless of whether it was apparent to the rest of us.

My first goal would be to assess the situation. I needed a cover, one where I would be able to ask questions without suspicion. "I'm thinking I'll go in as a journalist. Can you set me up with a profile? Freelance, online something."

"Journalist? Are you—"

"Make sure it's neutral."

A long pause. "Roger that."

"I already know wolves will be painted as the villains. But I can pretend like I want their opinions."

"Why do you like wolves so much?"

"I love all animals. It's just that wolves get a bad rap. Much more than other predators. They've become the center of a political hornet's nest. People just don't understand."

"Parents just don't understand…" he said with a cadence like it was a rap lyric.

"What?"

"Will Smith and Jazzy Jeff."

"You've lost me."

"You're not into nineties rap?"

"Um, no. Seventies and eighties sitcoms are my thing."

"Seriously?"

Eye rolls were abundant today. "Anything else?"

"Yeah, be careful out there. I've been reading up on it. The wolf haters honestly believe that eradicating all predators is, like, their God-given right or something. They think their way of life is under assault by environmentalists and the government. I don't think they're going to like any questions."

"People love when you ask their opinion. That's why I'm going in as a journalist. Neutral."

"About that—"

"Bye, Greg."

I pulled back onto the road and headed deeper into the heart of Lamar Valley, the spot in Yellowstone where wolves had first been reintroduced. Here would be the most likely place for me to catch a glimpse of one, or hopefully a pack. And find my old friend.

Once in the valley, I checked the usual, well-known wolf lookout spots. Several cars were parked in Long Pullout. The friend I was looking for stood a few yards off the lot, looking through a spotting scope he had mounted on a tripod. He was in his sixties, hair peppered with gray, and wore an green jacket with a fuzzy collar. Nothing had changed. He'd spent every morning he could in the park, watching for wolves, and today was no different.

I parked my car, got out, and approached him. "Wolves?" I asked.

Without turning to look at me, he pointed south, to the tree line. "On the ridge, about ten minutes ago. Haven't seen 'em since."

"Figures," I said. "My luck." I had just missed them because of Darwin Award honoree and the bison trample photo op. "How's the pack?"

"Good. Good," he said, nodding as he took another peek through the scope.

"John, it's me, Poppy," I said. "Maybe you don't remember, I did an internship here—"

He spun around, his eyes wide, and scooped me up in a big bear hug. "Poppy! I can't believe it's you." He let me go and stepped back to get a look at me. "Just look at you. All grown up."

"It's only been a few years. And I was in college then, technically already grown up."

"We all thought you'd be back the next year, full time." He pursed his lips, thinking. "Didn't want to come back to the park?"

"I'd love to, but now it depends on where I'm assigned. I got hired with Fish & Wildlife."

"Ah," he said, as though that delighted him. "Did you ever meet my wife Betsy?" He half-heartedly gestured toward a woman sitting in a lawn chair with a home-made, crocheted afghan wrapped around her legs and a paperback novel in her hands. She didn't look up. He looked back at me, and almost apologizing for her, explained, "We're here a lot now, since I retired."

"Congratulations." He had been a school teacher and spent summers here, watching every movement of the wolves and helping the biologists in their research. It was common for hobbyist naturalists to hang out in the park, help document sightings, and volunteer as docents. "I was hoping you could give me an update," I said. "On the wolves."

"You mean these wolves, or the fate of all wolves in general?"

I smiled. He'd always loved to talk about wolves most. "Sure, fill me in on everything you know. I'm working on a case, so go ahead and start from the beginning."

"Ah, the beginning." He gestured toward the expanse of land in front of us. "Wolves used to roam these lands, for tens of thousands of years. But, during the westward expansion of the nineteenth century, a campaign was mounted to eliminate them, by trapping, poisoning, any way they could. Not only were their pelts valuable, but ranchers wanted their livestock to be able to roam free.

"By the 1920s, wolves were all but gone from the landscape. Believe it or not, it was park policy back then to eradicate all predators. It was park rangers who killed the last of the wolves here. Their view at the time was to protect big game animals— the elk, moose, and antelope. They thought that if the wolves were allowed to remain, they'd kill off every last elk." He looked a little sad at the thought of the last wolf being killed.

My emotions were closer to mad. "That's ridiculous," I said. "They had evolved together. And nature has a way of keeping balance."

"Of course it does. We know that now. But the science of wildlife management was just beginning to be recognized. They also didn't realize how much of an impact removing wolves would have on the ecosystem. It's all part of the story, and a great lesson in conservation.

"You see, once the wolves were gone, the ungulates multiplied unchecked. They quickly overgrazed the range, and most noticeably, decimated the vegetation along the rivers, allowing erosion. They literally changed their own habitat, which caused starvation and disease to spread. So guess what? The park rangers once again brought out their rifles and had to cull the herds, shooting thousands of animals every year.

"They knew then that the answer was to bring back the wolves, but there were too many opponents. The hunters wanted the elk numbers high, knowing some would wander outside the park. They didn't want what they perceived as competition from the wolves for those elk. The ranchers had spent generations ridding the area of wolves. They were unmovable on the subject.

"So, to reintroduce wolves, the U.S. Fish & Wildlife Service had to make a deal. As soon as wolves reached a sustainable population, they'd be removed from the Endangered Species list."

I didn't realize that was the case, that the agency I worked for had made such a compromise. I wasn't sure how I felt about that. Taking them off the list would put them at high risk.

"They won and, in 1995, wolves were reintroduced to Yellowstone. We were fortunate enough to get a few from Canada relocated here. It was quite the process, mostly to make sure they didn't hightail it north once their paws hit the ground. Wolves have been known to do that. Like dogs that travel miles to find their way home."

"How'd they keep 'em from doing that?"

"Conditioning with food from this area. It mostly worked. Pretty soon they thrived and multiplied. Then guess what happened?"

"The ecosystem started to change again."

He nodded, happy to have a good student who was paying attention. I didn't want to burst his bubble by telling him I already knew a lot of the story. I was hoping to glean some information I didn't know. Like the U.S. Fish & Wildlife's deal. It bothered me. It bothered me a lot. I needed to find out more about it.

John continued. "They call it a trophic cascade—the trickle

down effect of apex predators. The wolves have reestablished a natural balance. The river banks have foliage again, keeping erosion at bay, and more, smaller animals have returned. The elk population is at sustainable numbers."

Now he was telling me the version explained in a video by Sir David Attenborough that has gotten over forty million views. I watched it before I'd left Montana, just a little extra research. Opponents say Attenborough's video is an exaggeration. Biologists say the truth is somewhere in the middle. Other predator populations—grizzly bears, cougars—have increased, as well as more hunting of elk just outside the border of the park. All factors. But wolves certainly have led the change.

"Today," John went on, enjoying having an audience, "there are about 108 wolves in the park among eleven packs and, as far as we can tell, they're doing quite well. As long as they stay within the boundaries of the park, that is. As soon as they set foot outside the lines, the locals shoot to kill. We've lost quite a few wolves that way in recent years, including two of our most beloved. They were famous." He shook his head in frustration. "They hate wolves. They're convinced that they kill for the pleasure of killing and live solely to terrorize ranchers and livestock."

I shook my head in frustration. That was the attitude I was most likely going to encounter in Idaho. "So much for science. Some people just want to believe what they want to believe. Too many werewolf movies."

"Too much history. And politics."

"That too."

CHAPTER 2

Winding my way through the Northwestern corner of the park, I was reminded of the incredible dominance of the Rockies. Every turn offered a view more awe-inspiring than the last. Purple mountains majesty indeed. I'd forgotten how breathtaking they are.

During my internship in Yellowstone, the mountains had been overshadowed by a summer fling with an emotionally unavailable park ranger named Ben. Driving with my windows down now, mountain air tangling my crazy red curls, it was hard to imagine how that could have been possible. Hormones... But I do have fond memories of a picnic by a mountain lake and several overnight hikes. And not so fond memories of Ben feeling me up before telling me he didn't plan on keeping in touch after the summer.

As interns, we'd never left the park. Now, as I crossed the state line out of Yellowstone and into Idaho, I wondered what Ben was up to these days. He'd been the withdrawn, silent type. Kinda like Dalton. Only Dalton was so much more... *Dalton*. Dalton wasn't an unfeeling jerk. In this case, maybe I was the cold-hearted jerk. I'd really hurt his feelings. Then he'd just gone. Without a word. *Where was he?* I know I'd been wishy washy about our relationship. Not because I didn't love him. But my job, our job, put us in danger and the agency forbids relationships for a reason.

Oh, to hell with it. I'd been round and round this so much my brain felt like it was stuck on the rinse cycle. As soon as he got back from god-knows-where, I was going to tell him how much I loved him and then...*I don't know*. Was that what he wanted? Something told me he wasn't taking time off to lie on the beach and contemplate our love affair. No. Reconnecting with his old SEAL buddies in Bimini had lit some kind of flame. He'd gone off to do something dangerous, something he didn't want me to know about. Without me.

Dammit, Dalton, where are you?

The sign read 288 miles to Payette National Forest. That's where I was headed. Just north of there to the little village of Elk Valley.

I pulled into a McDonalds to pee and get a super-sized ice tea. Seemed kinda counter productive, because I'd have to stop at the next one I saw to pee again, but a gal has to hydrate.

Back on the road, I cranked up the radio and tried to forget about Dalton.

The singer belted out a line, blah, blah, blah.

Where would he have gone? Why'd he leave without a goodbye? The thing that worried me most was his reaction. It was so unlike Dalton. At least the Dalton I thought I knew. Something had set him off.

Clearly the radio was not going to keep my mind off Dalton right now. I needed to talk.

I grabbed my phone and punched in Chris's number.

Chris was my best friend and always knew what to say. He'd distract me from this nonsense.

He answered on the first ring. "Hey girl. Can't stop thinking about Dalton, huh?"

"What? I—" I sighed. "Yeah well."

"Uh, huh."

"Actually, I have news. Hyland has made me point on this op. I'm the lead investigator."

"That's awesome!"

"Yeah, thanks."

"But that's not why you called. Not really."

"What? Of course it is."

"You know you can't lie to me. I see right through you. You can't get Dalton off your mind. We need to find that handsome hunk of SEAL meat."

"Find him? No. Um, you're supposed to distract me. Help me to stop thinking about where he's gone."

"Why?"

"Obviously, he doesn't want me to know. Or he would have told me."

He huffed. Typical. "Or"—he drew out the word for emphasis—"he wants you to go after him, like some kind of romantic, *Officer and a Gentleman*, finale scene, you know, march right in and sweep him off his feet, prove you really love him kinda thing."

"You've got to be kidding."

"No, I've been thinking about it. Omigod, if my man did that, strode through the factory and carried me away, I'd swoon like nobody's business."

"Yeah, but you're gay. I don't think it works the other way around."

"What? Of course it does. Everyone wants to feel loved, not have to guess. And you've been putting this man through the everlasting game show rounds of guessing. You need to step off that wheel and make a declaration."

"Are you taking something? Are you all jacked up on Red Bull right now?"

"What? No." He huffed. "Listen to me. Don't screw this up. We need to find him."

"Wherever he went, I'm sure he probably flew." I drew in a sharp breath. "Hah!"

"What? No. I can't."

Chris was a flight attendant with Delta Airlines. "You're the one who just said we have to find him."

"Yeah, so?"

"Can't you check flight manifests? Or something like that?"

"No. Technically, no. But maybe. If I pull a few strings. But only if he flew Delta. But I can't—"

"I don't want you to do anything that would risk your job."

"Well, that's refreshing to hear, my dear. Considering our history."

"Yeah, sorry."

"I'll call you back." The line went dead.

I cranked the radio volume higher. He was definitely jacked up on Red Bull.

As I drove into the town of Elk Valley, I felt as though I'd gone back in time about fifty years. Quiet. Peaceful. Green meadows stretched all the way to the mountains. I passed a shiny new Dollar General before getting to downtown, one block that consisted of a small grocery store, a drug store, gas station, a diner and two bars. A little church sat at the end of the street, alone, like the bothersome little brother. Priorities— praise Jesus but double up on Bud Light.

I took a slow pass, then, around the bend, I did a three-point turn in the road and headed back through. No motel. I'd have to find a lodge or something. The next town over was too far to drive back and forth everyday. I pulled to the side of the road and went into the diner. It was three o' clock. The waitress, a plump woman in her late fifties with hair pulled back into a bun stood over a tray of salt shakers, filling them one at a time.

She looked up from her work and an expression of mild surprise crossed her face, then was gone. "How can I help you?"

"I was hoping you could point me in the direction of a place to stay for a few days. Maybe a week or so."

She shifted her weight to one foot, rested her hand on her

hip. "Which is it? A few days? Or weeks?"

"Well, I guess I'm not sure yet."

She looked at me as if I'd asked for a ride in a DeLorean.

"I'm a writer...writing an article. I just got the assignment so I didn't have a lot of time to plan ahead." I frowned. "Do you know of a place?"

She shrugged. "Maybe Gladys. She rents to hunters. And since it ain't huntin' season, she might."

"Okay, great. Sounds good," I said. "How do I get there?"

She scrunched her eyebrows at me. "Hang on." She went into a back room, leaving me standing in the middle of the diner.

Moments later, she was back, an old phone held to her ear, the tightly-curled cord stretched from the kitchen. *People still had those?*

"She's standing right here. Shall I send her down?" she said, her eyes on me.

She nodded, then disappeared again, apparently hanging up the phone.

Back she came. "Yep, you can go down the road there"—she held up a hand and pointed—"about one mile, till you come to a crossroads. Take a right, then a left, and go another couple'a miles till you see a bright red mailbox. Turn in there. She's expectin' yah."

"Thanks," I said. That was easy. "And what's your name?"

She looked at me quizzically. "Oh, I'm Diane."

"Thanks for your help, Diane."

She was taken aback, as though no one had ever thanked her before. "You sure you got them directions?"

"Yep. One mile, crossroads, right, left, red mailbox. How's the food here?" I asked.

"Oh, it's good. It's good," she said nodding straightforward approval but her eyes revealed she was still pondering how I'd been able to memorize the directions.

"Great. I'll be back then. Thanks again."

She waved me off and turned back to continue filling the salt shakers.

I found the place without any wrong turns. They were great directions, actually. Gladys was a pleasant surprise. As spry as a spring chicken, her wispy gray hair pulled tight into a tiny bun at the back of her neck, she tsk tsked as I carried in my suitcase, trying to take it from me. I declined and hefted it myself, following as she took the stairs two at a time leading the way to my room.

"What'd you say your name was?" she asked over her shoulder.

Apparently, this is the type of place that didn't require introductions right at the front door. Or maybe she was so happy to have a guest, she'd rushed me in.

"I'm Poppy," I said as I stepped into my room. Simple. Cozy. The furniture was no-nonsense. Only what you'd need, a basic bed and six-drawer dresser made of well-worn wood. The top had three, nope, four doilies. One was hiding under the lamp.

"I don't get many guests this time of year," Gladys said, fluffing my pillow and straightening the bedspread. "And never young women. What brings you to Elk Valley?"

"Oh, I'm a journalist, working on a story about the wolves."

She froze. Her lips pursed and she furrowed her brow, clearly not impressed. "You one of them treehugger types?"

"Nope," I said. "I'm interested in all sides of the story."

"Mmm, hmm." Her frown deepened, not quite convinced. "Well, there's the bathroom anyway," she said as she turned away, gesturing in the direction down the hall, and left.

Well. I guess that's that.

After I closed the door, I placed my suitcase on the stand, unzipped it, and took out the few things to hang in the closet. The room was small but comfortable. In addition to the oak dresser, there was a little bedside table, also covered in doilies. *Decorative or functional?* Not my style but they seemed to suit the otherwise unadorned room.

I sat down on the bed and examined the map of Elk Valley. Not much as far as commerce. A lot of large ranches. Where to start?

If that diner served good food, I bet I could get a feel for the locals there.

After a quick shower, I grabbed my coat, locked the door behind me, and headed downstairs.

Gladys sat in a rocking chair in the living room, her nose in a book.

"I think I'll head back into town to that diner for dinner," I said.

She nodded without looking up from the book.

The main street had come alive. It was now lined with pickup trucks, all makes, from brand new Ford F-450s to old Chevys with rusted beds barely hanging on to the frame, all covered in too much dust to tell the paint color. My little rental car sat in the parking lot looking like a pony in a Clydesdale corral.

One mini motorhome was parked on an angle at the corner. Maybe I wasn't the only tourist in town.

As I entered the diner, amid the clank of dishes and silverware and bustle of the dinner rush, I felt the eyes on me. *Nope. I'm not from around here.* Since I'd left, the place had taken on the scent of home-cooked biscuits.

The booths along both walls were stuffed with men clad in flannel shirts and blue jeans. Families were seated at the three tables in the center of the room. One had a high chair pulled up at a corner, blocking the walkway and causing the waitress to walk all the way around to get to two of the three tables. Even the stools at the counter were all taken. *Food must be decent.*

Or the only the only food in town.

Hm. I spotted one booth with only three guys. *Here goes.*

I approached, giving them my best smile. "May I join you?

It seems the place is full."

My gaze fell on the guy who sat alone on the one side of the booth. His eyes lit up and he tried to rise to stand, but ended up awkwardly bent at the waist, stuck inside the booth.

I smiled and stifled a small giggle. I thought I might get more out of them if I acted a little cute. I hate that word to describe a woman, but right now, I needed the act.

He grinned and sat back down, yanking his John Deere hat from his head as I slid into the booth beside him.

"I'm Poppy."

He nodded, blushed a little. "Cody."

"Nice to meet you." I swung around to face the other two, blinking at them expectedly.

"Bobby," the one said. He was missing a front tooth.

"Bart," said the other. "Glad to meet yah."

"They're brothers," Cody told me. He eyed me up and down, not even trying to hide the linger on my chest. "You ain't from around here."

"Nope," I said. "So, what's good here?"

"Everything," Cody replied. He tapped his finger on the paper placemat in front of me. "That there's the menu." So, he was going to be the talker.

"Ah." I quickly glanced at the offerings. Nothing vegetarian. Not that I expected there would be. I scanned the breakfast lineup. Only available until eleven a.m. I scanned until I found something sure to not be dripping in meat grease. Saved by the kids' menu.

The waitress came up to our table delivering three plates of what looked like meatloaf slathered in gravy.

"Hi Diane," I said. That made the guys look at each other, wondering how I knew her name. She didn't wear a name tag. Why would she? Everyone from this small town knew her.

"Welcome back," she said. "What can I gitcha?"

"Grilled cheese sandwich, please."

"That all?"

"Iced tea?"

"Coming right up." She scribbled on her pad as she walked away.

"Where you from?" Cody asked, then shoved a forkful of food into his mouth.

"Michigan," I said.

"I always wanted to go there," Bobby piped up. "I ain't never been on a boat. I've seen pictures of that Mackin-nack Island."

"Actually, it's interesting, it's pronounced Mack-i-naw," I said. "Native Americans in northern Michigan thought the island looked like a turtle, so they named it 'Mitchimakinak,' meaning 'Big Turtle.' Then the French voyageurs who travelled the Great Lakes trading for furs gave it the spelling, then the British came along and added their two cents. Hence the confusion."

Bart and Bobby stared, open-mouthed.

Then Bart turned to Bobby, letting my information pass without comment. "Why would you wanna go on a boat?" he said, as though that's the first he'd heard of it.

"Cause I ain't never been on one, that's why." Bobby's attention came right back to me. "You been on a boat?"

"Yeah," I said. "My dad and I spent a whole summer on a sailboat when I was a kid."

Bobby's eyes grew wider. "No kidding. You get sick?"

"No. Not everybody does."

He frowned. He didn't seem sure that was right.

"Are you guys cowboys?" I asked, diverting attention away from me and back to them.

Nods all around. Cody responded. "We work out at the Split Fork."

"Is that a cattle ranch?"

He grinned and puffed up his chest a little. "Largest one in the county."

That must have been an impressive point.

Cody shoveled in another mouthful of food before he said, "What brings you to Idaho?"

"Oh, I came out here to learn about the wolves."

Bobby looked at Bart and Bart looked at Cody. "Why?" Bobby said. "You one of them wolf lovers?"

"No," I said, unsurprised by the question. "I just want to know what all the controversy is about."

"Controversy? Ain't no controversy." He shoved food into his mouth.

"Well, I know some people wanted the wolves reestablished in their natural range and some—"

"What the hell for? Why would anyone in their right mind wanna bring back somthin' we already took care of?" Bobby looked annoyed by the notion.

When interviewing, you have to be careful not to lead the interviewee. "Why do you think?" I asked.

"I got no idea." He responded shortly. "Only good wolf's a dead wolf."

"I understand. But why do you think *they* want them back?"

He shrugged. "Stupidity?"

Bart added. "Because they can't mind their own damn business."

I turned to Cody. "What do you think?"

Diane plopped my grilled cheese sandwich in front of me. "That going to be enough?"

"Yes, thank you." I picked it up and took a bite, my eyes on Cody.

He fidgeted in his seat. Either he didn't want to disagree with his buddies or he wanted to say whatever he thought I'd like to hear.

"Well?" I said with a mouthful.

"Well…" He poked at his meal with his fork. "I don't know. I ain't never had a run-in with a wolf, so I can't say."

I nodded. It was a fair enough answer.

I took another bite of my sandwich and thought about what I could ask that would get me some information but not rile them up to the point of clamming up. I glanced around. People were starting to congregate at the door, waiting for a table. A woman, sitting at the counter, was looking at me. When I made eye contact, she turned away. That was odd.

She was probably in her fifties, slim and fit, gray hair pulled back into a ponytail. She didn't seem to be with the people who sat on either side of her. Loners stood out in this small town.

I turned my attention back to Cody. "Do you think they should be allowed to live here in the Idaho wilderness?"

He shrugged. "I say, live and let live."

Bobby and Bart rolled their eyes. Bobby said, "God, Cody. A pretty girl sits down next to you and you turn into a damn jellyfish. What is wrong with you?"

That made Cody blush. Then he seemed to gather some courage. "Animals are all connected. Maybe they're supposed to be here for a reason." He paused and seemed to be searching for the right word, lighting up when he found it. "They're part of the ecosystem."

I had to admit, that took me by surprise.

"This is cattle country," Bobby said. "It ain't no e-co-sys-tem." He accentuated every syllable in the word, trying a little too hard to sound smart.

Cody shrugged.

To Bobby, I said, "How do you feel about bears and mountain lions?"

He gave me a half shrug. "Wouldn't wanna run into 'em up in the hills. But, whatever."

"What's the difference between—"

"They ain't wolves. That's the difference."

I nodded, tried to keep a neutral expression.

That was the bottom line. There was a special loathing reserved for wolves. Bobby was looking at me like I may join that list. He shook his head and turned back to his greasy meatloaf.

The boys gobbled up the rest of their meals, excused themselves, and paid their bills at the counter. Their abrupt departure made it clear to everyone in the vicinity that they hadn't appreciated the conversation.

I finished my tea and dug some money out of my purse. Diane came by and as she tallied up my bill by hand, she leaned in close and said, "Up the road about ten miles, on the right-hand side, is New Hope Farm. Nice sign. You can't miss it. Owner's name is Julie. You should go talk to her." She gave me a smile as she dropped the bill face-down on the table.

"Thanks," I said. "I'll do that."

When I left the diner, I dialed Greg and asked him to run a background check on those cowboys and any possible incidents at the Split Fork Ranch. Always good to know whatever you can about the players.

CHAPTER 3

Before dawn, I awoke, my body still on Eastern Standard time. The sun was pondering whether to come up, only a hint of light on the tips of the mountains.

I tiptoed to the kitchen to find Gladys already up, in a light cotton duster with a pastel floral pattern and fuzzy pink slippers, sipping from a mug of coffee, the newspaper in her hand.

"Good morning," I said.

"Breakfast?"

"Something light, maybe. Granola?"

Gladys scrunched her eyebrows together and assessed me as though she still wasn't sure if I'd arrived via flying saucer. "Eggs, bacon, and hash browns," she stated.

"I'll take one egg, scrambled. Thank you."

"That's why you're so skinny," she said, shaking her head and setting down her mug. She shuffled off toward the stove with the enthusiasm of Eeyore.

After eating the scrambled egg with homemade toast, then a quick shower, I set out for New Hope Farm. I figured if this Julie was a farmer, she'd be up. That's what they say right? Up before the dawn.

Long streaks of warm sunshine stretched across the valley, casting an amber glow. As I pulled into the driveway, the sun peeked over the hill and lit up the entire ranch, making it look as if it were coming alive before my eyes.

On the property were two old barns, a well-kept farmhouse, and a small fenced pasture to the south where two horses grazed. A few smaller structures were scattered about the plot of land, probably used for storing feed or equipment.

I parked next to the house, went up the two steps onto the porch, and rapped on the door.

Within a minute, the door flung open and a young lady with long, blond hair and thick eyeliner stood before me, a hairbrush in her hands. I guessed she was about fifteen. "Hello?"

"Hi," I said with a disarming smile. "I'm looking for Julie. Is she here?"

The girl spun around and yelled, "Mommm! Someone for you," then disappeared.

Teenagers.

A few moments later, a woman came to the door. "Yes?" She wasn't much older than me. Her sandy-blond hair was pulled into a pony-tail and she wore ripped jeans and a blue plaid, flannel, button-down shirt. This was a woman who wasn't a stranger to hard work. She looked as fit as any athletic trainer I've met. She greeted me with a welcoming smile.

"I hope it's all right to stop by at this early hour. Diane over at the diner suggested I talk with you. I was hoping to ask you about your experience with the wolves here in the area."

"Oh that," she furrowed her brow, looking tired. She stepped aside and gestured for me to enter. "Well, won't you come in?"

"Um, sure."

I entered, moving into the entryway far enough so that she could close the door behind me.

She headed for the kitchen, motioning for me to follow. "What did you want to know? The agent's already been by to do the inspection."

"Oh?" I said. *Inspection?*

"Of my chicken coop." She turned and stared for a moment. "I assume that's why Diane mentioned me, because of the recent incident."

"Yeah," I said. Seemed like a vague enough answer to keep her talking.

"Well, there's not much to tell." She gestured for me to have a seat at the kitchen table. "I was gone to Boise when they got in. Raised hell, and when it was over, they'd killed most of my chickens."

"Oh my gosh," I said, easing into the wooden chair.

She shrugged, but her body slumped with resignation. There was more to the story.

"Most of your chickens?"

"Yeah, I had a hundred and fifty. Only nineteen survived."

"I'm sorry to hear that. You're sure it was wolves, though?" Wolves weren't known to go after chickens. Foxes, coyotes, raccoons, yes. But chickens were an odd pick for wolves. They usually went after larger prey.

She nodded. "Can I offer you some coffee?"

"No, thanks. You can replace the chickens though, right? With reimbursement from the government?" Might as well get right to the heart of it.

"Well, yes and no." She thought a moment. "Who did you say you are?"

"I didn't. That was rude. I'm sorry. I'm Poppy. I'm writing about the wolf situation."

"Oh." Maybe it was my innocent face, but she seemed to accept that as enough of an explanation. "Did you want to see the coop?"

"Sure."

She grabbed a Carhartt coat off the hook behind the door and slipped on a pair of rubber boots. "C'mon."

I followed her out to the bigger barn, our footsteps leaving a trail through the tall, wet grass.

I love the charm of old barns, the antique structures both sturdy and timeless. The paint on this one was weathered, but the fieldstone foundation would mark this place for generations to come. For better or worse, it had become part of the landscape.

Around the backside of the barn we walked past an abandoned piece of farm equipment, possibly used for tilling, the grass grown up all around it. From the barn emerged a ramp from an elevated entry door, angled to the ground. About seven buff-colored chickens clucked and scattered as we approached.

"This is where they came in," she said, pointing at the ramp. "I must've left the door open or something. This time of year, when we keep the chickens in the barn, we close it every night, once they've come in to roost." She shrugged. "It was my own fault. I thought I had it secured." I could tell she felt a lot of guilt about it.

"I'm sorry that happened." Wolves going after chickens was really out of the ordinary, from what I'd read. Especially for a pack. They tended to avoid anything near regular human activity. I just couldn't get how odd that was out of my head. "And you're sure it was wolves?"

"Jack Wade came out and confirmed it. At least there's that. I'll get a little help replacing them."

There it was. The connection. Jack Wade.

"What does that involve? Replacing the chickens, I mean. Can you just buy more? Or are there other costs involved?"

Her sadness seemed to reach beyond that of a farmer having to replace her stock. "Well, the chickens are the core of our program."

"Program?" I asked.

"The New Hope Farm." Her face lit with an undeniable passion. "It's been my dream. I inherited this land a few years ago from my grandmother. I'm turning it into an organic community farm. We plan to invite at-risk kids from the city out for the summer to learn about where food comes from, what it means to work together, to dedicate yourself to something. It's been..." Her face started to flush.

"That sounds amazing," I said.

"Yeah, well, if I don't have the chickens, it doesn't work so well."

"How does having chickens help at-risk children?"

"Working together as a team with people who care about you is what helps the kids. But if we don't have a working farm, we can't offer that experience. See, it's not just about having a garden or some chickens. We believe in holistic farm management. We need every piece of the process."

"Holistic farm management?"

"We teach about symbiotic relationships and how a working farm, done right, can bio-mimic the natural world." She was talking with her hands, animated with enthusiasm. I could tell this was her passion. "Our farm is small, but it works because it's all about understanding the process of strategic disturbance."

"You've lost me," I said, though she'd caught my interest.

"Livestock can actually improve land health and rejuvenate the soil, if managed properly."

This was actually news to me. "I've always heard cattle trample the countryside, stripping it as they go."

"Exactly. The way most ranchers manage their herds, they have to spread out, keep moving, for continuous grazing. Unfortunately, that's not sustainable." She paused, as though she didn't want to badmouth ranchers. "Overgrazing has less to do with the number of animals on the land, and more to do with the amount of time the plants and soils are exposed to those animals."

"So, what are you doing that's different?"

"Rotational grazing. You cordon off temporary paddocks and move the cows every couple of days, *before* they overgraze. The short-term intense grazing allows stem regrowth, what you need for optimal nutritional levels. Then you bring in the chickens. The chickens do their job picking about for the insects and aerating the soil, encouraging the new growth. Their excrement is full of nitrogen, ideal for growing strong, healthy pastures. When the cattle move, the chickens do too, just one phase behind. And you keep the cycle going." She paused again, looking concerned. "Well, I don't want to bore you."

"Oh, not at all. That's fascinating. And you do all this work with at-risk kids?"

She approached the fence that enclosed the horses and leaned on the top rail, looking out over her pasture. I came and leaned alongside her, watching her think while she spoke.

"Our operation is quite small right now. I'm still trying to get things up and running. It's only me and Katy, my daughter, who you met at the door, and a few farmhands I've been able to hire part-time. We raised those chickens from eggs. It takes six months. The egg layers were just starting to produce eggs. That's why I was in Boise, to sell them at the Saturday farm market there and start the conversation about what we're doing here."

"Is there any reason you can't buy adult chickens with the reimbursement money?"

She shrugged. "From what I'm told, it'll be pennies on the dollar. Adult chickens cost a lot more than eggs or chicks. And there are other issues, too. They don't socialize well when they get put together as adults. It's best to raise them together from chicks. But most of all, if I don't know what they've been fed or how they've been cared for, I can't assure my customers they're organic."

"I see."

"So, we're set back six months. And with the seasonal nature of farming, it might as well be a year."

"I'm so sorry to hear that," I said. "I really am."

She pointed to the north. "On that side of the property we'd planned to build a rooming house, a dorm I guess you'd call it, for the kids. It's all been humming along on schedule. Until…" her eyes dropped to her hands, "until the wolves came."

I felt for Julie in her circumstance. She'd learned a lesson the hard way. When living on the edge of the wilderness, leaving the barn door open was like laying out the buffet.

She raised her chin and her eyes met mine. "You live and learn, right?"

I nodded.

"So, what are you writing about wolves for? Thesis?"

"No. I'm a journalist. I'm trying to understand all sides of the story."

"Ah," she said with a half grin. "Good luck with that around here."

"Yeah, I met some cowboys in the diner last night. They definitely had their opinions about wolves. As soon as I mentioned them, the gloves came off."

She turned to face me. "Be careful. Just the whisper of wolves around here stirs up some deep-seated anger."

A red pickup truck towing a horse trailer pulled into the driveway, the tires crunching over the gravel.

"Hm. I wonder why he's back," Julie said.

"Who?" I asked.

"Jack, the inspector." She headed to greet him.

I followed. *Well this is lucky.*

A man, whom I assumed was Jack, got out of the driver's side and another man, a Native American, slid from the passenger seat. I assumed he was a member of the local Nez Perce Tribe.

Jack had that look of a man who'd traveled every acre of the county on horseback. With slow, but deliberate care, he placed his cowboy hat on his head.

"Jack," Julie said, nodding in welcome. "And Mr. Whitefeather. Nice to see you. What brings you by?"

Jack pointed toward the hillside to the east. "We need to check on a collared wolf up that way. The signal has stopped moving."

"How can I help?"

"We're just asking your permission to cross your property

to get up there."

"Of course," Julie said. "You can park your truck next to the barn."

"Appreciate it."

They got back into the vehicle and slowly moved it forward.

"I'd really love to go with them," I said to Julie, trying to sound like the hopeful, aspiring journalist. "Do you think they'd let me tag along?"

"Probably," she said. "You know how to ride a horse?"

"Yeah, yeah," I said. I'd been on one. Briefly. Once. You just nudged them in the right direction and they knew what to do, right?

"I suppose I could saddle up Duchess for you. She could use some exercise."

"I would really appreciate that," I said. "You're so kind."

When Jack and Mr. Whitefeather got back out of the truck, Julie and I met them at the back of their horse trailer.

Julie introduced me, explaining that I was a journalist. "I didn't mean to be rude, before. Sorry."

I held out my hand. "It's so nice to meet you." Jack's handshake was firm, yet brief, while Mr. Whitefeather's was gentle, like a grandpa taking the hand of his youngest grandchild. Mr. Whitefeather had an aura about him, like he went through life counting his blessings every single day.

"I'd love to tag along, if you'll have me." I grinned, hoping.

Jack shrugged. Mr. Whitefeather smiled with his eyes.

"Great," I said before they could think of any reasonable objections.

"She can ride my Duchess. Give me a minute to get her saddled," Julie said.

I followed her into the horse barn. The scent of dry hay mixed with a hint of manure permeated the air. There were five stalls on each side, though I'd only seen two horses in the meadow. The other stalls had various items stacked in the corners—rakes, a wheelbarrow, plastic buckets, shovels. On a table between two stalls was a pile of carrots and a big bottle of what looked like horse vitamins. It was neat, well-kept, like the rest of the farm.

Two stalls had tack hanging on hooks at the gates and saddles on sawhorses. Julie went to the stall on the end and whistled for Duchess to come in.

She handed me a helmet. "Sorry. That's non-negotiable."

"No problem," I said. "I'd have asked for one."

With a soft clip-clop, Duchess stepped into the barn.

"She's a gentle mare. You shouldn't have any problems." Julie took a blanket from atop the saddle and placed it on the horse's back. "Isn't that true, girl?" she said to the horse in a calming voice.

I watched as she placed the saddle on Duchess's back, adjusted it carefully, running her hand along the shoulder, then the hip to be sure it was seated in the right place, then gently cinched up the belly straps. "When you get back, if you'd loosen the girth, I'd appreciate it."

"Sure, of course," I said. "That belly strap, right?"

Julie grinned. "Yeah. You sure you're comfortable with this?"

"Oh yeah," Poppy said, nodding.

She took the bridle and reins from the hook and held the metal bit in her hands, rubbing it. "It's pretty chilly out here. I just want to warm it up. I hate to put a cold bit in her mouth."

When she approached, the horse lowered her head and willingly took the bit. "She's such a nice horse," Julie cooed.

With the reins in her hands, Julie led Duchess out the door and into the yard. I followed, snugging the helmet chin strap and snapping it together.

The men had their horses ready to go.

Jack mounted his horse as Katy came around the corner of the barn.

"Mom! Mom! Something's wrong with Sannyu." With panic in her voice she motioned for her mother to hurry and then dashed in the opposite direction.

Julie dropped the horse reins and ran after Katy. Jack and I looked at each other and, recognizing the urgency of the situation, switched gears to see how we could help.

Jack dismounted and Mr. Whitefeather took the reins of all three horses, nodding for us to follow Julie.

As I rounded the corner of the barn, I saw Julie and Katy crouched over a wiry black and white dog. A border collie. He stood in an awkward sawhorse-type stance, rigid, his muscles stretched to the full extent they'd allow.

Jack reached for his cell phone and stepped away. I couldn't hear his words, only the urgency in his voice.

The dog's eyes showed his pain and fear. Katy knelt beside him and stroked his head. It triggered something, because the animal started to convulse and seemed to be struggling to get a breath.

"Mom! Mom! What do we do?!" Katy cried, pulling back her hand and staring in horror. The plea in her eyes made my heart stop. This dog was dying, violently fighting to stay alive.

"Dr. Mack will meet you at the Johnson farm," Jack told Julie. "It's closest and they have what he needs. You need to hurry."

"What is it?" Katy begged.

"I'll get the car keys," Julie said.

"Just go with your mom," Jack said. He picked up the dog and followed Julie to her car.

In moments, with Katy holding her dog in the passenger seat, Julie zoomed out of the driveway, throwing gravel onto the lawn.

I pushed aside my own feelings of desperation and panic. "What was that all about?" I asked, standing next to Jack, watching the car disappear around a bend.

He shook his head. "I'm not sure."

CHAPTER 4

Mr. Whitefeather handed me the reins to my horse, then mounted his own. His was a paint, and seeing him on the horse reminded me of Tonto on *The Lone Ranger* TV show I watched as a kid. The silly depiction of Native Americans was a little embarrassing now. We've come a long way but it's amazing how stereotypes can be ingrained in generation after generation. We've still got a long way to go.

"I'll pray for the dog. And the girl," he said once he was settled in the saddle.

I gave him a nod, indicating they were in my thoughts as well. *I'm going to pray for me on this horse too. Here goes nothing...* I placed my left foot into the stirrup and gave a little hop, cursing my height, or lack thereof, as I failed to get even close to pulling myself up and over. *Okay, too conservative.* I hadn't wanted to startle Duchess but realized I was going to have to really jump to get up in that saddle.

Reset. Good grip on the saddle horn and back of the saddle. Left foot in the stirrup. And jump!

I pulled myself up but didn't time my leg swing properly and launched myself belly-first onto the smooth leather of the saddle. My foot slipped from the stirrup and I slid right back off.

"Argh!" I exclaimed as I tugged my shirt back down. Duchess had barely moved and she looked back at me like she was asking what in the world I was up to. *I have no idea!*

Jack did not look impressed. "Have you ridden before? We need to get going and really don't need anything slowing us down."

My face was hot, probably about the color of my hair by now.

"I have but it's been a while. I've got it."

I put my foot back in the stirrup, swung my leg over the horse's back, and sat down on the saddle, causing the squeak of the leather as it stretched and adjusted. The design of saddles hadn't seemed to change much in the past two hundred years. I hoped they were comfortable for the horse, because they certainly weren't made for my butt.

Jack mounted his horse again and took the lead as we headed out. He was clearly annoyed with me and, frankly, I didn't blame him. It was probably going to be more difficult to get him talking now. *Dammit.*

Julie's ranch stretched across a lush valley. The hills sloped upward to the east, a gentle increase in elevation marked by the placement of the pine trees. In the valley, the pines were scattered, sparsely dotting the landscape. Higher up the hillside, they grew closer together. Above, a bright blue sky held one lone wisp of a cloud.

I drew in a deep breath of the cool, crisp air. *Mmmm, my kind of morning.* The clop-clop-clop of the horses hooves on the soft ground and the gentle squeak of my saddle lulled me into a peaceful trance. I was a cowgirl, out on the range. One with slightly damaged pride because I can't mount a horse, but yee-haw just the same.

When Jack came to a gate in the fence, he dismounted and swung it open for Mr. Whitefeather and me to pass through, then latched it shut again, and, with the grace of someone who'd been on a horse his entire life, he was back in the saddle and trotting past us, into the lead once more without a moment lost.

I gave my horse a nudge to come alongside him. "I understand there's been quite a few wolf incidents around here lately," I said.

He simply nodded.

"I was wondering how you know for sure that it was wolves."

"It's my job to know."

"No, I'm not questioning that. I'm wondering what evidence is required for you to confirm it. What do you look for?"

He looked over at me with a stoic expression. I couldn't tell if he was annoyed or really didn't have an answer. Finally, he said, "I didn't believe it myself at first. The rate at which this pack has been killing livestock, the level of depredation seems unprecedented. But all the evidence is there. Tracks, hair, bite marks. It's wolves." His answer was straightforward and matter-of-fact. Maybe too polished? I couldn't see his face to look for signs he was hiding something, but the lack of emotion in his voice told me he may be.

Part of his responsibility was to remove problem wolves, often by lethal means. I wondered what he thought about that part of the job. Him making a living murdering wolves was a sickening thought.

There was no doubt he was convinced wolves were the culprits. Or he was determined to convince me of that fact. My gut told me he honestly believed it. Yet something wasn't right. What motivation would he have to lie? The only answer I could come up with was for a kickback on the reimbursement payout. But Julie had said it was pennies on the dollar. It didn't seem worth risking his job or committing fraud. Unless the ranchers were offering some incentive of their own.

The simple fact remained: the number of attacks on livestock in this area was unprecedented for the known wolf population. It was possible that wolves had moved in from another area, but wolves are very territorial. Clashes with other wolves over territory is the most common cause of death in natural populations. The resident wolves would either run off the intruders or would be run off themselves.

"There's no doubt about it," he added, as though he knew what I was thinking. "Whether you want it to be true or not."

"I understand," I said, trying to sound curious and amiable. "Can you tell me a little more about the process? The way you investigate?"

"The scene?"

"Yeah."

"Well, wolves are endurance hunters, unlike, say mountain lions who hunt by ambush. Wolves force their prey to run and scatter so they can assess them for weaknesses, then wear them out so they're easier to take. With large prey like elk, during the chase, they'll attack the hindquarters and the flanks. They do the same with cattle and sheep. So, I look there first for slash and bite marks from the canine teeth and I measure them. Spacing of wolves' teeth are much wider than those of coyotes and their tracks are bigger, too. Often, when it's wolves though, they devour most of the carcass. If I don't have hindquarters left to examine, I'll check the bones. If they've been chewed or cracked open, it's likely wolves and I might get bite measurements from those, too."

"I see."

"The problem is, once wolves get a taste for livestock, they tend to go after it again and again."

"Can you tell me about Julie's chickens? What happened there?"

"What's to tell? She left the door open. Might as well have put out a neon sign."

"But is that typical of wolves, to go after chickens?"

"What do you mean by typical? With hungry wildlife, anything's on the menu. Especially with wolves. So, to go after chickens? Why not? Leaving the door open was asking for trouble. They had a heyday in there."

"Could it have been coyotes? Or a fox?"

"They left lots of tracks. It was wolves."

I nodded. Cold, hard evidence. "But how did they know to check the door that day?"

He shrugged. "Wolves are one of the most intelligent species on Earth, if you ask me. Maybe they'd been checking for months, patrolling the boundaries."

I couldn't help thinking of the velociraptors from Jurassic Park. I shuddered a little.

He continued, "Maybe the chickens sounded different that day, drawing them in. Maybe they got lucky. Who knows."

Someone does. Was someone purposefully luring wolves to attack livestock? Were they being set up as the fall guy?

Soon, we descended to the bank of a river I hadn't realized was there. From the farmhouse, it was hidden from view.

The bank was flat and low with a mix of gravel and sand, unexpected here in Idaho. To Jack, I said, "I always thought of Idaho as mountainous, with rocky rivers, you know, the perfect habitat for fly fishing."

He looked over his shoulder at me. "Mostly. It is upstream from here. But in this short stretch the river flattens out. It's shallow here, easy to cross."

He didn't slow but led his horse right into the river where the water didn't even come to the horse's knees. Mr. Whitefeather followed, with me right behind.

Once across, Jack turned to the northeast. He seemed to know right where he was headed, even though he didn't consult a compass or map.

"Are your collar readings that accurate?" I asked. "That you don't need to follow a signal?"

He nodded. "The newer collars are GPS, so yes. I know right where it is."

Technology was amazing. Some of the things Greg could do from his computer, sitting in an office in Chicago, blew my mind. Borderline creepy, but impressive nonetheless. Me, I preferred face to face interactions, being out in the field.

Except maybe not on a horse. I was still trying to channel my inner cowgirl.

Jack's cell phone rang, which jolted me back into the twenty-first century. He answered, said okay, then hung up. To Mr. Whitefeather he said, "The signal switched."

"Switched?" I asked.

"To a mortality signal," he said flatly.

"Oh." So, we were looking for a dead wolf to recover the collar. I don't know what I thought we'd been headed to find. A collar that had fallen off, I guess. This news upset me.

Jack must have seen my face. "If you want to head back, just follow the trail we left in the wet grass."

I shook my head. "No. I'm fine."

He frowned. No doubt he wasn't thrilled about having a mushy young *girl* to deal with.

Once across the river and through the budding willows that grew along the edge, the hillside turned steep. The horses handled the terrain without trouble. I simply held on, clenching my thighs and trying to assist by keeping my weight centered as we passed into the thick forest of lodgepole pine.

The piney scent in the air was both refreshing and invigorating. I tried not to think about the dead wolf. I had hoped I'd see a wolf while I was here. But I'd imagined a fleeting encounter, where our eyes met, and a primitive feeling of mutual respect passing between us before the animal loped off through the forest. That was a fantasy, I knew. Romantic notions. I was here to do a job.

When the terrain once again allowed, I brought my horse alongside Mr. Whitefeather. "What brings you out today with Mr. Wade?" I asked.

In his mellow voice, he said, "The wolves are my brothers. My charge."

"Your charge? How do you mean?"

"Our lives have always been intertwined. Together we have balance. But now, in modern times, the balance has shifted, and He'me has needed our help. We answer his call."

I could almost hear a mournful wolf call in my head and it gave me goosebumps.

"How do you answer?"

"Officially? In 1995, my tribe worked to convince the federal government to restore the wolf to its rightful place. We drew up an Environmental Impact Statement and, in response, we were granted $300,000 a year and given jurisdiction over wolf management here in Idaho. We've been dedicated to the process of recovery ever since."

"I know there are a lot of politics around the—"

Mr. Whitefeather gently shook his head. "Indeed. There are many opinions, many perspectives, most are all about the disagreements of men, not really about the wolf. But for the Nez Perce, it is different. Wolves are our brothers. While they've been gone, our sacred circle has been broken. What affects them, affects us."

We traveled on in silence for nearly two hours while I pondered Mr. Whitefeather's words—what affects them, affects us.

Finally, Jack slowed. "We're close," he said.

Mr. Whitefeather nodded and turned his horse from the single-file formation. I guessed we were to spread out to search.

I headed in a slightly different direction, but to be honest, I didn't want to be the one to find the dead wolf.

Within minutes, Mr. Whitefeather's calm voice traveled through the forest. "Over here."

I turned and headed in the direction from which his voice had come. When I found him, he still sat on his horse, looking down, a grim look on his face, sadness in his eyes. Jack had dismounted and was standing over the body, hands on his hips, shaking his head.

The wolf lay on the ground, not in a peaceful pose of having passed in its sleep, but as if frozen, every muscle clenched, locked so tightly death could not even release the animal from its last spasm. It was disturbing, unnatural.

I turned to the two men. "I've never seen anything like that," I said, horrified.

They had. I could see it in their faces.

"What is it?"

When Mr. Whitefeather answered, his voice sounded haunted, ghostly, as though he could see the future and it looked bleak. "Strychnine poisoning."

CHAPTER 5

"Strychnine? As in the way wolves were killed decades ago?" I shuddered. Death caused by strychnine is inhumane. The poison causes the most painful symptoms of any known toxin.

Jack nodded as he knelt next to the body. He rested his hand on the wolf's flank as if to feel for any warmth left.

"Is that legal?" I asked. I was a federal officer, and I had no idea. In recent years, the laws involving wolves had bounced across the books like pebbles skipping across water. It was hard to keep track of where they landed.

Mr. Whitefeather finally dismounted. He took a wooden flute from his pack and started to play a mournful tune that filled the forest with its sorrowful lament. It only lasted a minute, at best, but it set the tone. This wolf had died in vain, at the hands of some angry citizen who didn't care for the rule of law or the innocent other animals who might get into it too. To him, wolves were vermin to be eliminated. By any means.

But who? Ranchers and hunters alike shared the common hatred for wolves. They were the obvious suspects, but not the only ones. There were many people who feared wolves. People often fear what they don't understand. I see it all the time.

Jack carefully removed the collar, placed it in his saddle bag then rolled the wolf onto a small tarp. He wrapped it up tight, slung it over the back of his horse, and cinched down the straps, securing the bundle for transport back down the mountain.

He was taking the body to protect other animals that might feed on the carcass, like Katy's dog. "Do you think that's what happened to Sannyu? His muscles seemed to be involuntarily clenching."

Jack nodded. "It probably got into some carrion."

My heart sank. Poor Katy. How could this be acceptable? To set out poison, to indiscriminately kill? "Is the use of poison common around here?"

"Common enough," Mr. Whitefeather answered, his eyes held the weight of his heavy heart.

"Some people seem to have an excessive amount of anger directed at wolves. I don't really understand it," I said clenching my fists. I was angered and wanted to hear Jack's perspective. Wasn't he bothered by all this? Or was it all in a day's work for him?

Mr. Whitefeather answered instead. "The hatred of the wolf itself is born out of fear. But, like many things, it has become a symbol of a much greater issue—who controls the land, and therefore who controls the people who rely on it for their livelihood."

"I don't follow," I said.

"Nearly half of Idaho is public land and, for generations, the federal government has dictated how locals can and can't use that land. The reintroduction of the wolf, with its endangered status, was the last straw. Many see it as overreaching bureaucrats from the other side of the country ramming their policies down their throats, forcing them to conform."

I was impressed with his knowledge, not only from a cultural standpoint, but a political one as well. I knew I had to tread carefully with my next comment. "You're a Native American, supporting wolf reintroduction, which means you're on the side of the federal government in this."

His kind eyes took me in. "I know. Ironic, isn't it?"

The two men sat down in the grass and unwrapped sandwiches for lunch. Mr. Whitefeather offered me half of his, but I had no appetite.

"Are you sure?" he asked. "We won't get back until dinner time."

"I'm sure, but thank you," I said, pacing. I couldn't even sit down. Partly because my backside was already thoroughly saddle sore. The thought of getting back on the horse made me cringe. Setting out on an eight-hour horseback ride my first day was a brilliantly impulsive decision. I tried to rub my aching haunches without the men noticing. I wasn't sure my bottom would ever forgive me.

Once they were finished with lunch, I successfully mounted Duchess, this time using an old tree stump as a mounting block, and we headed back down the mountain with a dead wolf draped over the hindquarters of Jack's horse.

As we neared the halfway point to the river, we came across two cowboys on horseback. Jack brought his horse to a halt. Mine stopped without me having to do anything. *Such a good horse, Duchess.*

I didn't recognize the men. They weren't in the diner last night. They were both young, about the same age as Cody and the brothers I'd met. They tipped their hats in greeting. "Mr. Wade," one said.

"How're you boys?" he responded.

"We got a stray calf. You hear or see anything up that way?"

"You from the Johnson ranch?" Jack asked, though it was clear by his tone that he knew they were.

They nodded.

"Why would you think the calf was up this way?"

"We're just lookin."

Jack and Mr. Whitefeather exchanged a look but seemed to accept the response.

"Best of luck, boys," Jack said and nudged his horse back

into motion. As I passed the two cowboys, their eyes latched onto me and followed as I continued on. *If looks could kill.*

"Wolf lover," one said, loud enough for only me to hear, the words dripping with disgust.

I spun in my saddle. He flashed a half grin and spit on the ground, clearly amused with himself.

My blood hit flash boil. *What the hell?* Had Bobby and Bart been shooting their mouths off about a skinny redhead in town asking questions about wolves? I thought I'd remained neutral, careful in my approach. Apparently not.

Why did a few simple questions stir up so much vitriol? It was clear, I had inadvertently stepped on a hornet's nest. That wasn't going to help me get the answers I needed. Maybe Jack had heard about me before even meeting me, too. That could be why he was so matter-of-fact with his responses. He was prepared.

I frowned. Hyland had put me in charge of this operation. Maybe I wasn't the right temperament for this kind of nuanced investigating. I had underestimated the depth of hatred of wolves out here. I needed to get a handle on this.

When we got back to the farm, there was no sign of Julie or Katy. Jack and Mr. Whitefeather kindly helped me remove the horse's saddle. I turned her out in her pasture and made sure the water bucket was filled.

After they'd watered their horses and loaded them back into their trailer, Julie pulled into the driveway. Katy got out of the car and went directly into the house.

Julie turned off the ignition, then got out and stood with her arms crossed as if hugging herself for support, watching her daughter run off, concern on her face. I approached and she sighed as she turned to me. "We still don't know much of anything, though the vet felt we probably got there in time."

"That's encouraging," I said. I had no idea what a veterinarian could do to counter the effects of strychnine poisoning, it that's what it was.

"He put him under anesthesia and the muscle seizing stopped but…" She shook her head. "I don't know." Her attention went back to the house and her daughter.

"I really appreciate your loaning me Duchess, Julie. Jack and Mr. Whitefeather helped me take care of her," I gestured to them as they walked up to us, "but, I should head out. I don't want to be in your way—"

"Oh no. Please stay. Jack, Mr. Whitefeather, you too. Please stay for dinner. I think it would be good for Katy. Besides, I might not have enough eggs to sell, but I have more than the two of us can eat alone. Please. Really. It would mean a lot."

The men looked at each other and nodded. It seemed like it would be rude to turn down a home-cooked meal in these parts. And Julie didn't seem to want to be alone right now.

I nodded in agreement and asked, "Is there anything I can do to help?"

"No, but thank you. I'm going to get Katy busy in the kitchen, keep her mind off things."

My phone rang in my pocket, startling me.

"Perfect timing," she said. "Take your phone call and then c'mon inside."

The men followed her in.

It was Chris.

"Hey, Chris. What's up?"

"I found out."

Dalton. He knew where Dalton had gone. My heart fluttered. "And?"

"He's in Africa."

"What? *Africa*? Are you sure?"

"Well, he bought a plane ticket there."

"Why in the world would he—" *No way.*

"What is it?"

"You don't suppose…"

"What? Do you think—"

"He's gone to find out about my dad."

"We don't know that."

"Why else would he go there?"

"I don't know. There are lots of reasons to go to Africa. Lions and elephants and those super sexy South African accents."

I could almost hear his mischievous smirk at the thought of rippling muscles in the African sun.

"But we both know Dalton."

"Well, you do. You really think he went to investigate your dad's death?"

"In Bimini, when I asked Jesse about Africa, he said Dalton had already asked him about it. He tried to cover, said they talked about it in general, his time there, when he was in the Marines. But I got the feeling Dalton had been specific."

"What if he was? I mean, let's just say for a moment, that it's true. Maybe he wants to find out what happened and put things to rest for you. That's admirable."

"Yeah, I guess."

"What's bugging you?"

"What if he gets in trouble? What if he asks the wrong questions? What if he asks the wrong people? It could be really dangerous. I can't ask him to do that."

"You didn't. He went on his own, remember?"

I sighed and ran my hand through my unruly hair. "But I hate the idea of him over there alone, without backup, poking around. Who knows what kind of trouble he might stir up. He doesn't know the whole story. I need to stop him. Can you get me on a plane?"

"What? Are you kidding? No. Poppy. Listen to me. You just got to Idaho. You've been put in charge of this operation. In *charge*. Poppy, don't you realize? This is what you've always wanted, remember? To be—"

"Yeah, but—"

"Yabbut nothin'. Dalton is a big boy. He chose to go without you and he chose not to tell you. And for good reason."

"What's that supposed to mean?" There was a long pause. "I'm doing it again, aren't I?"

"Poppy, I love you. So I'm just going to say it. You're way too emotional about the whole thing with your dad. It's too personal. If I had to guess, I bet Dalton knows that and he's been concerned you might someday go yourself, all half-cocked. He probably wanted to get ahead of it."

"Get ahead of it?" Had he? Would he? When I'd asked Jesse about Africa when I first met him, did that make Dalton think I was planning something? And he thought…what? "This is crazy."

"People in love do crazy things."

"Chris, I don't know what to do."

"I do. Stay right where you are. Do your job. Do it well. Dalton will be back soon. Then, you can ask him. Simple."

"Yeah, sure, simple." *Not.*

I disconnected and dialed Dalton's number. It went straight to voicemail.

Do my job. Simple.

Yeah right. Dalton was on the other side of the globe, doing god-knows-what. I paced to the fence and back. If I went to Africa, how would I even find Dalton?

Crap!

Do my job. Okay, fine. Focus. Run point. What did I know so far? Not much. Someone was poisoning wolves. I didn't trust Jack because I was sent here to investigate him and I didn't like the attitude of those cowboys. It all started with Bobby and Bart. What I needed was someone on the inside, poking around, over at the Split Fork Ranch.

I dialed Mike's number.

Mike was on my team, but he and I had a bad history. He'd tried to push me out on our first operation together and it hadn't gone well. He'd been driven to make senior agent and nothing was going to get in his way. I ended up having to rescue him and save us both. His ambition had almost gotten us killed. Trust was shaky between us, but I'd worked with him since and I needed him for this mission.

He answered on the second ring.

"Hey, Mike. It's Poppy. I've decided your cover. We need a cowboy on the inside. Rustle up some leather chaps and roping skills and c'mon out here."

"Are you fricking kidding me?"

"Well, maybe not the chaps. Or the roping. In fact, I really don't know what modern cowboys do. But we need someone over at the Split Fork Ranch. It's the biggest around, so there's a good chance if you—"

"If I what?"

"Show up looking for a job."

"And *you've* decided that I'm supposed to play a cowboy?"

"You've bragged about your acting skills before and I've seen them first hand." I tried to keep the disdain out of my voice. "We need someone to get close to the cowboys over at the Split Fork Ranch. The attitude of—"

"Yeah, ask Tom."

"No." My blood pressure was climbing into the triple digits. "I'm point on this operation and I'm telling you that's the role I need you in."

"So, Hyland made you point, huh?" He made a tiny huff sound. "What you got Tom doing? He'd be much better at it."

"I have something for Tom." I didn't yet, but I wasn't going to tell Mike that. I couldn't let him tell me how to run my show. "We all have to play our part." My hand went to rub my sore bottom.

"Well, it's not gonna fly. I've never been in the same county with a horse, let alone been on one."

The image of him uncomfortably perched in the saddle made me grin. "Well, there's a first time for everyone."

"You know what I think? I think you're doing this on purpose, to get back at me."

I sighed, loudly, so he could hear it through the phone. I didn't need this crap. "You know what I think? I think you need to get your ass on a plane and grovel, beg, bribe, whatever it takes to get a job working at that ranch."

I hung up.

CHAPTER 6

With my hand on the doorknob, I paused and took a deep breath. *Dammit Mike. Just do your job. Why do you always have to be such an ass?*

I entered the house where the scent of sautéed onions lingered in the air. "Mmm. That smells heavenly," I said as I kicked off my shoes.

I poked my head around the doorframe to the kitchen. Katy was at the stove, stirring something in a saucepan. Julie bustled about the kitchen, taking plates from a cabinet and digging silverware from a drawer.

"Let me wash my hands and I'll take those," I said. "I'm not much of a cook, but I know how to set a table."

She waited for me to scrub up, then gladly handed them over, and I carried the place settings into the dining room, where a large, rough-hewn wooden table had been pushed up against the wall. Jack and Mr. Whitefeather were already seated, their hands wrapped around mugs of coffee.

Julie followed right behind me carrying a hot glass dish, straight from the oven. She set it in the middle of the table, removed her red plaid oven mitts, and shoved them under her arm. "Egg casserole," she said. "Be careful, the dish is hot."

Katy came in behind her with a serving spoon and another dish. "It's a sauce to drizzle on top."

They both found their chairs and I sat down next to Katy.

Julie's phone rang. She sprang up from the chair. "That must be the vet."

Katy sat up straight-backed in her seat, her worried eyes on her mother.

The four of us waited, expectantly.

"Okay, okay," Julie was saying to the caller. "Oh my. Okay."

She disconnected and sat back down. "Dr. Mack says the tests confirmed, Sannyu got into some poison."

Katy drew in her breath. The look on her face made me want to strangle someone, anyone, everyone who's ever used poison to kill anything. How could they be so cruel?

"But he said not to worry. He thinks we got him there in time and he'll be okay, with no long-term damage."

Katy's face tightened, her lips pinched together. She was trying not to cry.

"That's great news," I said, trying to reinforce what her mom had said while feeling relieved myself.

Julie touched her daughter's face and turned her to look into her eyes. "He's going to be okay," she reassured.

Katy nodded, her emotions on the verge of bursting free.

"Sannyu is a beautiful name," I said. "Where did that come from?"

Katy seemed to need some oxygen before she could answer. She huffed, then smiled. "It's Luganda for joy."

"Luganda? As in the language of Uganda?"

She nodded, but her mind was on her dog, not answering me.

Julie answered for her. "Katy's youth pastor went on a mission trip to Uganda two years ago. It was a once-in-a-lifetime experience for him and he's been talking about it ever since, teaching the kids about the situation there, trying to plan a another trip to go back. She's been hoping to raise money to go with him."

"I bet," I said. "That would be amazing." It would be. Africa. Dalton was in Africa. I shook the thought away. I couldn't think about that right now. Jack. I needed to find out more about Jack.

Julie took hold of the serving spoon. "Let's dig in before it gets cold."

We each handed her our plates, one at a time so she could serve us, and then she filled her own plate.

I took a bite. "This is delicious." It truly was. "The eggs are rich and creamy. I've never tasted eggs like this."

"It's how I feed them." She popped a forkful into her mouth.

Jack and Mr. Whitefeather both mumbled agreement with full mouths.

"I don't understand!" Katy yelled. The damn had finally burst. Her face was pink with hot anger. "Why would someone poison my dog?"

Jack answered, his voice calm. "I'm sure they didn't mean to. They put the poison out for the wolves."

Was he defending them? I tried to keep my eyes from narrowing at him. *Neutral, Poppy, neutral.*

"So, they just stick poison out anywhere?" Katy was having none of it.

Jack nodded, unfazed. "I'm afraid so. Some people want 'em all gone and they take matters into their own hands. Your dog probably got into some carrion they'd left behind. Something like that."

Her lip pushed up into a pout. "I hate it here. I want to go back to Boise."

"I know you do, honey," Julie said. "But you haven't given it a chance."

"A chance? Why can't you see? We don't belong here. They don't want us here. All our chickens are gone. And now this." She rose, sending her chair sliding across the wood floor with a screech. "You're just too stubborn to see it." She stomped out of the room.

Julie held her face in her hands, rubbing her temples. "I'm

sorry gentlemen, Poppy. She's just…"

Mr. Whitefeather, with his calming voice said, "It's been a rough day for her."

Julie sighed and nodded.

I hated to be insensitive to Katy's grief, but this was my opportunity to press Jack. "You suspected it was poison," I said to him. "That's why you called the vet right away."

Jack didn't deny it.

"Has this been going on for some time? Or is it a recent response to the increased depredation?"

Jack shrugged. "Both, I'd say."

I had to give Jack credit for one thing, he seemed to take my questions in stride. Seemingly unshakable. I pushed on. "Any suspects?"

"Too many. And it's not that I don't care, but it's not within my job description to investigate it."

"But investigating the increased depredation is, right? So, what do you think is causing it?"

"Honestly, I don't know. I've been asking myself the same question."

"Has the wolf population increased around here?"

He glanced at Mr. Whitefeather. "Not that we've been able to record."

"Has something happened to the prey population to cause the wolves to change their behavior and go after livestock?"

"It's not that they've changed behavior. Wolves will go after livestock. That's why the reimbursement programs are in place. What I think you're getting at is, can we identify one single cause? Not that we're aware of."

He was answering everything perfectly, like he already had an attorney on retainer. I had more questions.

"Has the local pack recently lost an alpha?"

Mr. Whitefeather shook his head and answered for him. "We don't know that either. We don't have any alphas collared. Only a few betas."

Jack said. "I see where you're going. If an alpha is lost, packs tend to splinter. It's certainly possible."

"Maybe it was one lone wolf that went after Julie's chickens? Individual wolves, split from a pack, would become more desperate, right?"

"That could be exactly what's happening, but we can't confirm that yet either."

"What *can* you tell me?"

"That there has been a significant increase in depredation in this region in recent months." He looked me dead in the eye as if he knew I didn't want to believe it. "And that it's definitely wolves."

I couldn't put my finger on it, but something just wasn't right. I took another bite of my egg casserole. *What would Dalton say?* He'd tell me wishful thinking doesn't make something true. If all the evidence points to wolves, then it's probably wolves. But it just didn't feel right.

I shook my head. "So, the locals will continue to put out poison?"

"Probably."

"Aren't there non-lethal ways to deter wolves? I mean, there has to be something? Some way that people can get along with wolves."

"Keeping the barn door shut's a good start," Julie said with a self-deprecating giggle.

"Yes, but cattle and sheep—"

"There are," Jack said. "There've been some experiments with strategies like using fladry, light and sound devices at night, and increasing the number of guard dogs. But it's all about incentive, and right now, the ranchers don't have much. They can shoot a wolf on their own property without a license. They can shoot a wolf that's actively molesting their livestock anywhere. And there's the reimbursement. Adding non-lethal deterrents are costly and add to their workload."

"Not to mention," Mr. Whitefeather added, setting down his

fork. He'd cleaned his plate. "There's a five-month open season to hunt wolves that will likely get expanded." He sighed. "At least this isn't Wyoming, where 365 days a year, wolves are classified as shoot-on-sight vermin."

I shook my head. It was true. Idaho and Montana had at least put some sort of wolf management plan together to maintain the required minimum sustainable populations, but Wyoming had one plan all along—as soon as wolves were removed from federal protection under the Endangered Species Act, they'd be annihilated.

"Thank you for dinner," Jack said, pushing his empty plate toward the center of the table. He seemed to be done with my interrogation.

But I had more questions—like what is fladry, anyway—but it was obvious Jack was tired and I'd pushed my luck this far.

Julie rose from her chair. "It was my pleasure. Please stop by again soon."

The men graciously slipped out the door.

"Let me help you clean up," I said.

"No, no. Katy can help," she said, shooing me with her hand.

"Katy's had a long day. I don't mind. Really."

Julie's shoulders slumped and she dropped the perfect life facade. She was tired and was done pretending she wasn't.

I gathered up the dirty plates and headed for the kitchen. "I'll wash."

At the sink, I turned on the hot water, squirted some dish soap into the stream, and swished the dishrag around in the soapy water to get it wet.

"Do Jack and Mr. Whitefeather come by often?" I asked, scrubbing a plate.

"I just met Jack for the first time when he came out to inspect my chicken coop. But he knew my grandma. She's the one who left me the farm."

"Did she live here alone?" I asked, making conversation.

"Yes, right up until the day she died."

"I'm sorry for your loss," I said, hoping to be some comfort.

"I miss her. This farm…" Her eyes filled with the mist of nostalgia. She shook her head as though trying to shake the memories away. "I used to come out here for the summer when I was a girl. My grandmother was not a warm person. She was a cattleman's wife. Strict. Stern. But I loved the ranch, the wide-open space, the long days in the sun, the work, feeling like I had accomplished something every day. Now I'd hoped to give other kids the same chance."

"It's absolutely beautiful here."

She took a dish towel from a drawer and started to dry the plates. "Yeah, I just…I hope it works out."

"Katy will come to appreciate it, too. Maybe she just needs a little time."

Julie nodded, kept her eyes on the towel in her hand.

"I wanted to ask you, if you don't mind, now that the men are gone, did you find anything odd about the wolf incident?"

"Odd?" She focused on the dish in her hand.

"Yeah. Like, had there been anything that happened prior to that? Anything that might have given you reason to be more cautious?"

"I don't know what you mean."

Neither did I. I was fishing.

What had Katy said? *They don't want us here.* "What did Katy mean? Earlier? When she said, 'they don't want us here.' Who did she mean?"

Julie shrugged. "You know, teenagers. So dramatic. They never feel accepted and the world is against them."

"But I got the sense that maybe—"

"It was wolves. I can tell you don't want it to be, but it was."

Okay. That was a little odd. "It's not that, it's just—"

She looked me right in the eye. "I can prove it."

I stared back. "Okay."

"Come with me. Let the dishes sit. C'mon."

She spun around and headed for the living room.

I rinsed the soap from my hands, dried them with the towel, and followed her.

She fired up a laptop computer that sat at an antique desk in the corner. Once it was on, she clicked on a file on the desktop that launched a video player.

"See for yourself," she said, pushing back the chair as she rose, offering me the seat.

The video was taken of her barn with a thermal-imaging camera. The image is dark blue. A few seconds in, a wolf enters the frame—a glowing red form in the shape of a wolf. Then another, then another. They head right up the ramp, single-file, into the coop. Then all hell breaks loose. Chickens fill the frame in a frenzy of flapping wings—blurs of red and yellow and green—as they try to take flight, scattering with no place to go as the wolves leap, snatching them out of the air. She clicked off the video, ending the disturbing sight.

"See? It was wolves."

I stared at the frozen frame for a moment. I didn't want to believe it. There was a part of me that held out hope, that there had to be some other explanation. But to have this kind of evidence, well, it was indisputable. I mean, thermal-imaging video that—"Wait, how'd you get that?"

"What do you mean?" She seemed to shrink back a little.

"A video like that. Thermal-imaging is very expensive. Why would you have it set up to record the barn to begin with?" I rose to face her. "Unless you suspected something."

She stepped back, her eyes wide with fear.

"Julie, what's going on?" I pressed.

"Nothing."

"What are you afraid of?"

She shook her head. "Nothing."

"Why would you have a thermal-imaging video camera set

up like this?"

"I didn't. It was…my aunt. She was worried about me and Katy being out here alone, out in the middle of nowhere, as she put it. She set up some security things around the house and stuff. It's nothing."

I nodded, letting her think I'd accepted her explanation.

But it most definitely wasn't *nothing*.

CHAPTER 7

I got back to my room at Gladys's place after dark. Nestled in her rocker with a ball of thread in her lap, she worked a tiny shuttle in her hands, tying the thread into fancy knots.

"What are you making?" I asked as I slumped onto the couch.

"I'm tatting," she said. "Making lace."

"Ah." That explained all the doilies.

"How was your day, dear?"

"All right, I guess. Though I spent eight hours on a horse, which was at least seven hours too many."

This brought a smile to her face. "Yeah, it takes some getting used to."

She set the tatting aside and pushed herself up and out of the chair. "I'll get you a cup of tea."

I was too tired to argue.

"Are you getting anywhere with your writing?" she asked from the kitchen.

"I learned a lot today, if that's what you mean."

Her head poked around the end of the wall. "Like what?"

"Like people around here don't like wolves much."

"Mmm hmm," she confirmed before disappearing again.

I got up and joined her in the kitchen. "How do you feel about them?" I asked.

She looked at me skeptically. "You gonna quote me in your

article?"

"Not if you don't want me to."

She shrugged. "I guess it don't matter no how. Ain't nobody I know likes 'em."

"Why do you think that is?"

The teakettle whistled. She poured the hot water into a mug, tucked a tea bag in and slid it across the counter to me.

"They was gone for good. Don't know why folks in Washington think they ought to be brought back."

"I see." I was too tired to dig any further. Gladys wasn't a suspect in any wrongdoing. Just uninformed, and if my intuition served me, unwilling to look at the science. How was I going to convince the locals like her to get along with the wolves? That they don't have to kill them to protect their livestock? That there are other ways. I know I was here to investigate Jack but I couldn't help feeling there was something bigger going on and the wolves were in danger.

"Thanks for the tea," I said. "I think I'm going to call it a night."

"Suit yourself," she said and went back to her tatting.

I fell fast asleep but tossed and turned all night.

Dalton was in Africa. *Africa.* Why didn't he tell me he was going? Why would he keep it from me? The last time we'd talked, he was mad as hell at me. Or hurt, I guess, if I was honest. But that wasn't a reason to disappear for two weeks without a word.

Who was I kidding? It probably had nothing to do with me. Maybe he was going to visit an old SEAL buddy. Or go on a safari. Or...*I don't know.* It didn't matter. After how I'd treated him in Bimini, I was sure our relationship was over. I'd never seen him so upset. But what did he expect? His ex-wife popped up out of nowhere, an ex-wife I didn't know existed. How was I supposed to react?

It didn't matter. He had said he loved me. That should have been enough for me.

Now, he was in Africa to find out about my dad. I was certain of it. And probably to put some space between us for a while. Chris was right. Like always. *Dammit*.

Just before the sun rose, I gave up on sleep and dragged myself out of bed. I rolled out my yoga mat and lay down in savasana pose, also known as corpse pose. A yoga teacher once told me she would bow in awe if I spent the entire class in that pose. At the time, I thought that seemed odd. It wasn't difficult to lie there, like I was dead. But over the years, I came to understand the wisdom. Who can lie still for that long, with only their thoughts?

My thoughts this morning were zinging around inside my skull like pinballs, setting off bells and gongs—ding, bong, bing. Dalton. This case. Jack. Julie. Katy's poor dog. Bobby and Bart. Those cowboys who had sneered at me out on Julie's land. Gladys. A pack of wolves at the center of it. Mike and his damn contempt. *Asshole*. I needed to get Tom out here, too.

But for what? I barely had a case. Jack wasn't lying. Julie's video proved it. Though the fact that she had the video was odd. Who points a thermal-imaging camera at a barn?

None of this made any sense. It didn't surprise me though. Hyland probably had some ulterior, top-secret reason for sending us here that she wasn't about to reveal, just like in Bimini with the dolphins.

No matter. I had to do something for these wolves. There was a reason they were attacking livestock. Were they being driven out of the woods? Was there more going on than someone poisoning them? That was bad enough, but I had a feeling that wasn't the extent of the danger.

This was much more than a simple increase of depredation. But what? I had a whole lot more questions than I'd come here with. I needed to talk to Hyland again.

I unplugged my phone from the charger, found her number,

and hit send. She was two time zones east, so it wasn't too early to call.

She picked up right away. "Agent McVie. Have you settled in?"

"Yes, ma'am."

"And?"

"And I've found there isn't a lot of sympathy for wolves out here. I started asking a few easy, neutral questions. Some cowboys got quite vocal, even outright brazen with their opinion. I've called Mike in to apply for a job over at one of the ranches so he can poke around." *And I had to threaten him to do it.*

"I assume he wasn't amenable."

Wasn't amenable? Was that politically correct code for being an ass? "He was concerned that he had zero experience with horses." *Did he whine to her about his assignment?*

"Ah," she said. I swear I could hear her smile. "Well, he's an experienced agent. He'll figure it out." That was encouraging.

"I stumbled into meeting Jack Wade. I spent the entire day with him yesterday, actually."

"How did that happen?"

"I went to investigate an incident of wolf depredation at a chicken farm. He showed up with another man, Mr. Whitefeather of the Nez Perce tribe, asking to cross the owner's property to look for a collared wolf. They were heading out on horseback, so I asked if I might tag along, and Julie, the property owner, kindly offered her horse."

"And?"

"And we found the wolf. It had been poisoned with strychnine. Ms. Hyland, someone is poisoning the wolves."

"Did you get any vibe about Wade?"

"Did you hear what I just said? Someone's poisoning the wolves."

"Do you think it's Wade?"

"I don't know. I don't think so but he's very careful with his responses. I'm not sure who it is, but I'd like to—"

"Doesn't matter. Not our concern. Focus on the sites where Wade has confirmed wolf kills and approved reimbursement."

"But poisoning wolves is criminal."

"Actually, it's not. Wolves have been delisted. Any illegal take is under the purview of the state. And in Idaho, at best, it's likely a violation of a pesticide law. Forget about it."

"Forget about it? You can't be serious?" My hands were shaking.

"You're there to investigate Wade." She sounded like my high school calculus teacher when I'd argued that I'd never use all those crazy, complicated equations in real life.

My lip quivered. "And I am. But they must be related."

"Do you think Wade's involved in something or not?" Her question was firm. She didn't want me out here any longer than necessary.

"Well, I…I don't know yet." *Dammit.*

"Well, it's your job to find out. Go do it."

I held my breath. "I need Tom. I mean, I need him to—" how could he help weed through the political nonsense, help sort out the bad apples, what was I reading about? "—to pose as a rep of a non-profit, here to help the ranchers develop non-lethal ways to deter the wolves. That way we'll have another angle to interview them. He can hit all the ranches and, in his pitch, get a feel for who is open to the concept and who shuts him out right away." Now I was babbling.

"If that's what you think is the best use for him."

"I do," I said, almost defiant. Then a thought struck me. "I still have Dalton to assign. When he gets back, of course."

"Fine, just get some answers about Wade," she said and hung up.

Really? No goodbye?

No confirmation on Dalton…? What the hell?

Was this really about the wolves? Or was there some internal political thing going on with Hyland? Something about Jack

Wade? Or the federal agency he worked for?

I tossed the phone on the bed, frustrated. Why in the world did she put me in charge of this operation? I don't do politics. Give me a bad guy, and I'll take him down. But this? *Ugh.*

I called Tom, filled him in on the details of what I needed from him, the research he'd need to do (like find out what the hell is fladry), then stepped into the shower and let the hot water soak my hair and run down my back, soothing my aching muscles.

I hadn't been point on this operation for forty-eight hours and I already wanted to scream my head off.

I used the day to do my own research on the history of wolf politics in the nation and in Idaho. What a tangled mess. Just as John in Yellowstone had claimed, the U.S. Fish & Wildlife service had been right in the middle of it all. It was Fish & Wildlife who'd led the reintroduction of wolves into Yellowstone, garnering agreement by negotiating with state governments—Montana, Wyoming, and Idaho—with the promise that they'd delist wolves from the Endangered Species list as soon as there was a sustainable population.

The problem has been the astronomical power of the anti-wolf lobby here in the west. Agreeing on the definition of "sustainable" has been at the core of the fight, and time and time again, policy decisions have been based on politics, rather than science.

It was making my head hurt.

At three o'clock, I decided some exercise would do me good. I needed to get out of the house. Maybe a short hike around Gladys's property. I needed to think.

Her house was an old-style timber frame that clung to the hillside, overlooking the valley, where, I assumed, her cattle had grazed. The house faced west, and the afternoon sun shined in the windows, lighting the rooms with a warm glow. I found her in her rocker. When I asked about a hike, she rose and went to the window, pointing westward. "Follow the old fence line," she said. "Keep to the north. You'll see a path."

I laced up my hiking boots and set out.

The air was damp with the scent of spring and the sunshine felt warm on my shoulders. I set a pace to get my heart rate up yet enjoy the scenery.

Once I got to the bottom of the hill and set out across the meadow, I heard the distinctive whistle-warble of the western meadowlark in the distance. This was just what I needed to clear my head. And stretch the sore muscles in my *gluteus maximus*.

Hopefully, another full day of horseback riding wasn't required again in the near future.

The image of Mike on a horse, trying to rope a steer, made me grin. *If you hadn't pulled that asshole move in Chicago, you'd be point on this op.*

How would Mike handle all this? Would he be sending me to that ranch to get a job as a cowgirl? Would he call in Tom to talk non-lethal methods with the ranchers? Would he even care about whomever was poisoning the wolves? Probably not.

Who cares? It's my op. My dad's voice echoed in my head. *Don't second guess yourself. You know what to do. Do what's right for the wolves.*

One thing I knew for sure, whoever the cruel bastard was who was killing wolves with strychnine, was going down. If I had my way, he was going down hard.

I followed the fence line as Gladys had described and as I turned back to the east, I saw movement up ahead. I came to a halt. Three elk stood in the field in front of me, munching on the spring grass. I froze in place, not wanting to disturb them.

The air was cool enough that I could see their breath when they exhaled. As they dipped their heads, an ear would twitch, or the tail flicked. Then one head came up—a young male. He had antlers, though small, in full velvet. He looked around as he chewed, then dropped his head to grab another mouthful.

All three had the scruffy look of their shaggy winter coats shedding off. It made me want to grab a brush and go at it.

The bull lifted his head again and looked right at me. His nostrils twitched. He was trying to get a scent, but I was downwind. I stayed still, watching. They were beautiful and deceptively docile. Almost as large as a horse, and as agile as mule deer, a full grown elk could plow me down without missing a step.

I slowly retreated, leaving them in peace.

The hike had done me good but I still hadn't been able to escape my doubts. My thoughts raced around my head at the speed of a Tasmanian devil. I needed a beer.

Gladys gave me directions to the Buckend Roadhouse, a honky-tonk down the road, outside of town. I figured I could grab a bite and a beer and see who else I could meet, check out the local crowd.

The gravel parking lot was huge. I wondered if it filled up on a Saturday night and what kind of crowd that would be. Today, there were quite a few vehicles for 5:30 on a Wednesday.

As I entered through the solid pine door with an elk antler for a handle, I had to let my eyes adjust for a moment to the darkness. Toby Keith trilled on from the jukebox about beer for his horses. A waitress zipped by me. "Sit wherever you want."

Some couples sat at tables. Four men played pool in the corner. Three single men were spaced out at the bar. Near the jukebox stood two young men I recognized. The two who'd been looking for the lost calf.

I shuffled across the wood floor, through a scattering of peanut shells, to a bar stool with my name on it.

The bartender came right over. "What can I getcha?"

"Sierra Nevada?"

"Bottle or tap?"

"On tap? Nice. Yes, please."

In moments, he'd set a frothy malt beverage in front of me and disappeared again. I drank down two gulps. *Ahhhh.*

I slowly looked around. No one here looked like anyone I'd seen at the diner last night. The two cowboys took notice of me, though. They headed my way. Each took a stool on either side of me and leaned in, purposely invading my space.

"Howdy. What brings you in tonight?" one said with a smirk, the one who'd smirked at me in the woods.

"Tired from all that ridin'?" the other asked.

They weren't flirting. They were trying to intimidate me, the way they were leaning in so close, from both sides.

"I very much enjoyed the ride. It was a beautiful day," I said, faking a coy grin.

"That so?"

"What are your names?" I asked. I'd get Greg to work right away on their rap sheets, if I get a little more specific info. These two creeps probably had long ones.

"I'm Carl," said the smirker.

The other attempted a smirk. "And I'm Don. What's your name?"

"Poppy."

"Well, ain't that cute."

"You're the first to ever notice." I batted my eyelashes sarcastically.

He pulled back, eyeing me, clearly unsure if he was supposed to feel insulted.

Then his hand came down onto my forearm and he clenched it tight. "Do you think you're funny?"

I tensed. I'd like to have twisted his arm back and slammed it into his face. But it wouldn't serve me to make a scene. I had to act like the innocent journalist.

"Please don't do that."

"Do what?"

"You're hurting me."

"Oh this?" He squeezed tighter.

Asshole.

"I don't like gettin' sassed."

I'd had enough. "Sassed? Who says that? Were you born in 1850?"

His eyebrows pinched together. He didn't get my point. "You got a mouth on you."

Yeah, and a black belt.

"You'd do well to move along, little girl."

"Don't you mean skedaddle?"

His face went blank. He didn't have a clue how to respond.

"Boys, let the lady be."

I spun to see a man standing behind me, arms crossed, a look on his face that meant business. He must have been someone, because the boys skedaddled real quick-like.

He stepped toward me, his expression one of concern. "Are you all right?"

"Yes, thank you," I said, watching them go.

"Don't mind them. They won't bother you again." He flashed a grin.

"Because you say so?" Who was this guy? He looked like a young Bradley Cooper, with that same heart-melting smile.

He held out his hand. "Exactly. I'm Casey. Can I buy you another—what is that?" He pointed at my beer.

"Sierra Nevada."

"Excellent choice." He gestured for the bartender to bring another. "You don't have to worry about those boys because they're all bluster anyway."

I had a feeling they weren't, and he was downplaying his ability to keep them in check. Casey. He had striking blue eyes and a strong jaw, peppered with ruggedly sexy stubble.

He laid his hand on the stool next to me. "May I join you?"

"I'd like that," I said.

He eased onto the stool and propped his elbow on the bar so he could comfortably face me. "You're obviously not from around here and this isn't exactly a tourist destination. So, what brings you to Elk Valley?"

I looked him right in the eyes. "Wolves."

"Ah. Let me guess," he said without missing a beat. He looked me up and down. "You're not a hunter. For one, it's not hunting season, but also, you're not wearing the requisite pink camo."

That made me grin.

He took the opportunity to look me up and down again. "You'd look good in it, by the way." He cocked his head to the side as though truly pondering the question. "You can't be a biologist."

"No?"

He shook his head. "They all wear glasses."

"Really?" I grinned wider.

"Oh yes. It's all the studying."

"I see."

"You don't work for the government."

I raised my eyebrows. "And how do you know that?"

"Government employees are too stuffy. No. You've got your own style."

"And what's my style?"

"If I had to guess, I'd say you're a writer."

I nodded. "Good guess." I leaned closer, looked up at him through my eyelashes. "Or word has already gotten around town?"

That made him grin. "What are you writing about?"

"I'm a journalist, actually. I'm curious about human-wolf interactions. What all the fuss is about."

"Who do you work for?"

"I'm freelance. I write for some online pubs, stuff like that."

"And that pays well?"

I shook my head. "Not really. That's why I hang out in bars like this, hoping someone will take pity on me and buy me a beer."

He grinned. "Wow, the boys were right about one thing. You

are sassy."

I just smiled. If he only knew the half of it.

"I heard you were out looking for a wolf with Jack Wade yesterday. You find it?"

"Wow, the grapevine around here is quite something."

"Indeed."

The big wooden door swung open and a couple walked in. The woman was the same one who'd sat alone at the counter at the diner, the one who'd been eyeing me, I was sure of it.

Right behind her, a herd of cowboys came in and disappeared into a back room.

"So, you might be interested to know that this weekend is the county stock show. If you want to get a feel for the culture around here, that's the place to be."

I turned back to him. "Culture?"

"You said you're interested in human and wolf interaction. It's all part of the big picture."

This Casey was a bright man.

"People come from all over the county. There'll be contests, and vendors, and all kinds of stuff you might enjoy, like the bull riding and—"

"Bull riding? Do they still do that?"

"Still? Are you kidding? It's a professional sport."

"I've always wondered. What do they do to the bull to get him to buck like that?"

He shook his head. "You don't want to know."

"Well, I don't get it. I mean, it doesn't look that hard."

He threw his head back and laughed. He took my hand in his, rose from the stool, and gave me a gentle tug. "C'mon with me."

"Where're we going?"

"Not far. You can bring your beer."

"All right then." I picked up my beer with my free hand.

He led me into the back room where the gang of cowboys had gone. The tables were arranged around a ring filled with cushions, and at the center, a mechanical bull.

He bowed and gestured toward the bull.

I shook my head. "Oh no. Nope."

"Truly, it's not that hard. I mean, it's only eight seconds."

"Are you mocking me?"

"Not at all. You just strike me as the kind of gal who'd take the challenge. I didn't want it to pass un-offered."

"I see." I stared at the fake, headless bull. How hard could it be? Really? "Sure, why not?"

Casey's grin widened. He led me to the bull, helped me climb on top of it, showed me how to place my right hand, palm up, under the handle, then left me, moving to stand next to the man at the controls. When I looked his way, he gave me a thumbs up.

By this time, a flock of cowboys was already forming to watch the show. I gazed out at my audience. *What is a group of cowboys called anyway? A gaggle? A horde?*

I probably shouldn't be doing this, bringing attention to myself.

The bull made a creaky noise and slowly started to move. I gripped the handle and held my left hand up in the air like I'd seen bull riders do in the movies. It was for counter balance. I could do this.

As it rocked forward and back, I moved at my hips to counter it, keeping my torso upright. I was still sore from horseback riding, but no way was I going to let that stop me.

Forward and back, forward and back, then it kicked to the side, throwing my weight the other direction. I held on. Forward and back, forward and back, then the kick. I was ready for it.

Forward and back, forward and back, then the kick. I countered. Then I felt the backend swing and dip, throwing me the other way. I had nothing to brace against and I was airborne. I landed on the floor cushion with a thump.

The men snickered and cheered. "Get back on!" "Don't let 'em throw ya, little lady."

I should stop now. I stared at the ceiling. *Yep, you've already made a scene.*

I got to my knees and crawled back up onto the bull. Once my hand was cinched in where it belonged, I gave the man at the controls a thumbs up. The bull started to buck again, forward and back. I clenched my thighs together. That was the key. *Keep your core tight.* Maybe lean more forward? *I don't know.*

Forward and back. The cowboys cheered me on. Forward and back, then the kick. I countered. The bull swung left then right so fast, I went flying off, landing on my side.

"Ooooh," the cowboys cawed in unison.

I got up, brushed myself off, and got back on. Casey was grinning at me. I looked out at my audience. The woman was there, watching me. That woman again. Who was she?

The bull started up again, tossing me from side to side. I hung on, countering this way, then that, then it was as though the floor collapsed and I went straight down. The bull had swung right out from under me.

I lay there for a moment, staring at the ceiling, listening to the merry band of cowboys cheering, knowing they were taunting me. To them, I was a dumb little girl from the city, trying to play with the big boys. Just the persona I wanted. Not a threat.

Casey stood over me, offering a hand. I took it and he hauled me to my feet.

"Want to take another go at it?"

"No." I straightened my shirt. "You got me. I admit it. Maybe it's not as easy as it looks."

CHAPTER 8

After two frustrating days of knocking on doors, asking to interview anyone who would be willing to talk about wolves, I got used to getting the door slammed in my face. I was glad the weekend had come, and I had the county stock show to attend.

The parking lots were jammed with livestock and horse trailers jockeying for spots closest to the barns. I'd never seen so many pickup trucks in one place. Apparently, no one in rural Idaho drives a sedan.

I found a parking spot near the back of one of the lots and headed to the fairgrounds.

As I entered the first barn, the odor of hay and livestock, all crammed into one building, was overwhelming. At one end of the building, an auctioneer yammered away over the low roar of people chatting as they looked over the animals being paraded, one by one, before potential buyers. Others moseyed among rows of painted red fence enclosures, about six by six, that held sheep. Some had ribbons tacked to their gates or on poster board at the back of the pen.

The next barn held the cattle. The one after, pigs.

I made my way through the barns to an outdoor area where tents housing vendors had been set up in rows. A group of protesters were gathered at one end carrying picket signs. One read, "Welfare ranching kills wolves." Another read, "Public lands don't belong to ranchers." It was a small group, no more than twenty people, but they were here, nonetheless.

Another contingent milled about on the other side of the area—nearly three times the size—protesters wearing camouflage clothing and hunter's orange vests. A little girl carried a sign that read, "Will there be any elk left when I grow up?"

Now I might get somewhere. I held my cell phone in my hand and, acting like I was checking for texts, slyly sniped pictures of as many protesters on either side as I could to identify later.

I assumed the protesters came out because the governor was due to make an appearance this afternoon. Again, I was reminded, the wolves were at the center of the politics here.

The vendor booths ran the gamut of feed supplements to cowboy boots, hunting outfitters to land conservation organizations. I walked through, taking my time, then came to a halt in front of a booth that promoted Wildlife Services, a division of the Agriculture Department—the government agency that Jack Wade worked for.

I glanced at their literature. Every pamphlet on the table was about dealing with conflict between livestock and wildlife. There was information on wildlife damage management, on wildlife hazards to farmers, migratory bird damage, invasive species damage, wolf damage, lethal control of wildlife (by many ways including the use of M-44 sodium cyanide injection capsules), disposal of wildlife carcasses, wildlife disease, traps, baiting, and, there it was, pesticide use.

Was Jack Wade aware of the strychnine poison being used in the area because he'd administered it himself? It seemed Wildlife Services, ironically named, offered nearly every conceivable way to be rid of wildlife that one could think of.

I backed away. This wasn't the place to delve into that line of questioning and my blood pressure had risen high enough to run a freight train engine.

I moved along through the booths—farmers insurance, tools, non-stick fry pan demonstrations, cowboy hats, toy tractors, dog food. There was a booth for the group, Idaho for Wildlife, promoting the Idaho Coyote and Wolf derby. A hand-written sign hung at the back of the tent, "Wolf hunt! $1000 in prizes!" I came to a halt.

"What's this derby?" I asked, trying not to stare at the photos clipped to a string by clothes pins. Included in the pictures was a pile of coyote carcasses in the back of a pickup truck and a wolf hanging from a pole. I was disgusted by the blatant celebration of death.

The two men who stood behind the table looked at me, unsure at first of how to answer me, someone who didn't look like they would be interested in partaking. Maybe I should have worn pink camo. Finally, one answered, crossing his arms, "Well, little lady, it's a weekend hunting competition for wolves and coyotes."

No shit.

The other man stuffed some chewing tobacco into his mouth.

I stepped closer. "What do you mean by competition?" I doubted he meant the wolves and coyotes would compete as hunters, but I wasn't going to argue semantics with this guy.

The second man spoke while positioning the tobacco with his tongue. "The one who kills the most wins."

"Well, the most coyotes," the first man clarified. "Then there's the prize for the biggest wolf. You should c'mon out." He looked me up and down skeptically. "We got special trophies for the women's and kid's divisions."

So, this is an organized killing contest, I wanted to say. "So, this is a special weekend event, like a festival?" I said instead.

"Yeah, people come from all over the state. It's a lot of fun."

"I'm confused," I said, tapping my finger on a flyer on

the table. "This says the organization's name is Idaho for Wildlife."

"Yep, that's the name of our group. We fight against all them animal rights and anti-gun organizations who are trying to take away our rights and freedoms under the Constitution of the United States of America."

"They wanna take our guns," the other added, for emphasis, then spit tobacco juice on the dirt floor.

I moved along, keeping my mouth zipped shut, wondering how a non-profit organization can legally get away with having such a misleading name.

Yeah, McVie. You're doing great. Just keep your mouth zipped.

A little self-talk goes a long way.

The next booth interested me. It was for the Wild Mustangs of Idaho. A sign read, "Keeping the wild in our wild horses and wild places." The young lady, adorned with a leather vest and cowboy hat, was happy to tell me all about their work. "The iconic wild mustang," she said, "is a symbol of the American way." She went on to explain that there are six designated wild horse herd management areas in the state of Idaho as well as a permanently protected wildlife preserve.

I didn't know that.

A few booths down, I saw a familiar face. Casey, with his tan skin and sparkling blue eyes and easy smile. I paused, causing the couple behind me to run into me. With my apologies, I stepped to the side. He was a handsome man. If I worked that angle, I could probably get a lot of information from him. But it didn't feel right. I had no idea what was going on with Dalton. But why should that matter? I had a job to do. I needed to get information. Any way I could.

I moved toward him.

The sign above Casey's booth read, "Elk Valley Lodge— Guided Outfitting." His gaze caught mine and he smiled.

I smiled back. "So, this is your business?" I said, pointing at the sign.

"Yep. We don't get any local business, per se, but it's always good to remind our neighbors we're here. They make referrals."

"I see." I saw the flyers on the table at the front of his booth that read, "Stop the Wolf Hunt."

"And it's convenient to make a political statement, too." I grinned again.

He grinned back. *Damn, he was handsome.*

"You didn't mention this when we met at the Roadhouse."

"You skedaddled before I could."

"Uh-huh. You enjoyed that little encounter I had with those men."

He shrugged.

"If you own—are you the owner?"

He nodded.

"If you own a hunting guide service, why wouldn't you want a wolf hunt?"

"I don't want wolves. I want more elk. It's that simple."

"Is it?" I said. "So then are you saying be rid of wolves all together?"

He gave me a half shrug, that kind men give when they know what a lady wants but think they can weasel out of whatever it is.

"What are you saying, Casey?"

"I'm saying that the way decisions are being made now aren't based on good science. Sure, one could say more wolves mean less elk. I'd like more elk and less wolves. But the government *letting* us hunt them isn't going to have any effect. I say cut all the regulation."

I'd heard this argument before – hands off my land, hands off my guns, hands off my right to murder animals because they're on my land and I'm using my gun.

I leaned on his table and raised one eyebrow, "But you want the big bulls, right? The trophy elk, right?"

He stared, a hint of a grin forming. He knew what was coming and leaned in toward me as though he were listening intently. His eyes crinkled with humor, telling me he wasn't offended by my willingness to banter. I was having fun in spite of the fact that we were on different sides of the argument. So, I kept going.

"Aren't they the healthiest and strongest members of the herd? Predators naturally target the easiest, least dangerous prey—the young and old, the sick and lame. Therefore, the impact of wolves to healthy adult male elk, or mule deer, or moose for that matter, is minimal."

He leaned back and put his hand on his chin like he was considering my position. After a moment he put his pointer finger in the air as though he had an ah-ha thought. I snorted at his antics.

"But…" He leaned in again and I was distracted by the scent of his cologne. Was that cologne? Casey smelled like clean air and hard work and sunshine and whatever makes attractive men smell so damn good. "I'm looking at the long-term viability of my business. Those young elk grow up to be big elk. But more importantly, you used to be able to look down this valley and see herds of 'em. In the hundreds. Not anymore. Not since the wolves were brought back."

I shook my head slightly so I could think without being distracted by how good Casey smelled. "If it's big herds you want, then shouldn't you be calling for fewer cattle and sheep? Truly, one could argue that livestock have as big, or bigger, impact on elk populations. They dominate this landscape to the detriment of almost every other species that depends on grass to survive. They leave little left for your elk to eat."

"I see you've been doing your homework."

"No argument then?"

There was the slightest hint of a head shake. Then his eyes held mine. "How about I buy you another beer later? I'll be at the Roadhouse when all this closes down. Everyone will. It's the party of the year."

I gave him the same shrug of non-commitment. "Maybe. See ya." I turned and walked away. I had to be careful with him. His masculinity was magnetic. He was sharp. And he knew everyone in this small town. He probably knew exactly what was going on. But why would he tell me? That was the million-dollar question.

I made my way toward the food vending area. The odds of finding a vegetarian option, even a salad, were a million to one, but I had to try.

As I crossed a main thoroughfare, Julie and Katy were walking through in the other direction with Sannyu. I waved and they moved through the crowd toward me.

"How's Sannyu doing?" I asked, bending down to pet him when they got close.

"Okay," Katy said. "He's not one hundred percent, but Dr. Mack said I could run him in the agility competition. You should come watch."

"Sure. I'd love that."

Katy smiled wide. "He's going to win."

"It's in the main arena," Julie offered. She looked at her watch. "In one hour."

"I'll be there, cheering him on."

CHAPTER 9

The main arena was surrounded by rows of bleachers, all under a huge pavilion. I was handed a flyer that listed all the afternoon events: kids swine show, breeding heifers, sheep shearing contest, and the dog competitions, which included stock dog trials, agility, and the extreme event, whatever that was. After that, at five o'clock, the rodeo events started. There would be steer roping contests, barrel racing, and dancing horses. The grand finale was, of course, bull riding. *Maybe I should enter, ha ha ha.*

I found a seat in the bleachers and munched on a bag of cinnamon almonds while the next event started, the stock dogs.

A temporary chute was set up and three cattle brought into the arena. The announcer's voice came over the loudspeaker, "These talented canines will demonstrate their agility, intelligence and athleticism as they carry out their handler's commands."

A man entered at the other end of the arena with a dog, some kind of mixed breed, cattle dog/border collie, maybe.

The man whistled and the dog sprang from one side of the small herd to the other, nipping at their heels, forcing them closer together and moving toward the chute. The dog would sprint, then skid to a halt in the dirt, then sprint again. It had some subtle intimidation techniques that weren't apparent to me, but they seemed to work. The cattle didn't like it one bit. They tried to head butt the dog, then would spin and kick. The dog, somehow, deftly missed each attempt by the steers, wearing them down, until the cattle gave in and slowly filed into the chute, causing the crowd to cheer.

The cattle were let out again, and another contender entered the ring. This man looked familiar to me, but I couldn't place him. He wore a green plaid shirt and a monster belt buckle, and, of course, the requisite Stetson hat. The walk could most definitely be described as a cocky swagger.

As he crossed the arena with his brown and white border collie, I caught sight of Julie, leaning on the fencing. Next to her was the woman who'd been staring at me at the diner.

I rose from my seat. This was my chance to find out who she was.

"Oh, hi Poppy," Julie said as I eased next to her at the fence.

I nodded, then looked right at the woman. "Hello."

Julie paused, ever so slightly. "This is Raina."

I held out my hand. "Poppy, nice to meet you."

"Likewise," Raina shook my hand and tilted her head slightly in acknowledgement.

Neither said anything more, but Julie was clearly uncomfortable, looking straight ahead as if she didn't want to encourage conversation.

"Are you a farmer as well?" I asked Raina.

Julie jerked back. "She's...she's my aunt. Remember I mentioned my aunt?"

"Oh yes." *The one who put up the thermal-imaging security cameras.*

"She's just in town for a few weeks or so."

"You must really enjoy staying at the farm," I said, testing. "It's so beautiful there."

Raina didn't show the slightest hint of unease. "It is. But when I visit, I stay in my van. I like my own space." Her gaze held mine like she was testing me too.

"Oh, I see." I didn't, but I would. The presence of this so-called aunt was too much of a coincidence.

The man handling his dog started shouting orders, left, right, push, push, in a low, angry voice.

I turned my attention to the arena. "He seems harsh," I said. He really did. There didn't seem to be an ounce of encouragement exuding from that man, only a threatening presence. I felt bad for the dog even though he was doing a good job.

"Yeah, that's Denny." Julie didn't seem to be a fan either.

"You know him?"

She cringed, ever so slightly. "He's my neighbor."

I nodded. There was something there. Didn't seem like they had a very positive, neighborly relationship.

In all, there were seven stock dog trials, five were dogs owned by Denny. "He's got some well-trained dogs there," I said to Julie.

"Yeah, that's what he does. He has the biggest kennel in the state of Idaho. Livestock guard dogs and herding dogs. He breeds some different combinations to get the best traits. He always wins at the shows."

The workers quickly disassembled the chute and carried the agility obstacles out into the ring. Soon, the handlers filed in to walk the course before their trials. Katy scanned the audience and found her mom at the rail. She waved from the ring.

"Oh, I hope this goes okay. It's been rough week," Julie said.

Raina placed her hand on Julie's arm and gave her a supportive squeeze.

Katy would compete third. The first two dogs ran the course, making pretty good times, according to Julie. Though one knocked a pole down and would lose points for it.

When Katy's time came, she entered the ring, put Sannyu in a sit, then took off for the first obstacle at a full run. Sannyu launched from his sit on her command, straight for the jump.

Then he was up and over the A-frame, through the tire, and into the weave poles. We cheered like crazy.

He rounded the corner, following Katy's commands, jumped, then jumped again, onto the teeter-totter. He was off again, but as he came out of the tunnel, he slowed. Katy urged him on and he kicked into gear again, but as he took the A-frame again, he hesitated and it cost him time. Once he crossed the finish line, he was visibly huffing and then he simply lay down.

Katy gave a cry and fell to her knees, scooping him up in her arms.

Julie took off for the arena at a dead run. I followed, Raina behind me.

"He's going to be okay," Julie was telling her. "He's just tired. Still recovering. But Dr. Mack said he'd be okay."

Katy nodded, but worry lined her forehead and tears were welling in her eyes. It was clear she wasn't sure she could believe her mom.

"Let's just take him back to his kennel. We'll walk slow, give him a chance to catch his breath."

Katy nodded and set Sannyu back on his feet. He looked steady and she started to lead him away. When Julie moved to follow, Katy spun on her and snapped, "I can take him."

Julie nodded, wringing her hands.

"She's just upset. She wanted him to win, so she'd know he was okay," Raina said.

Julie nodded. "I know."

"I tell you what," I said. "I have to head that way in a minute. I'll check on her. Okay?"

Julie nodded in agreement.

I followed her back to the rail. "Where's Raina?" I said when I noticed she was no longer with us.

Julie shrugged. She didn't seem concerned. Her mind was on her daughter.

We watched the next contender, then I left her to check on Katy.

The kennels were in a small barn a short walk from the arena. I entered and had to make my way through a maze of horse tack and other people before I found the dogs in the back corner. Katy was still there, talking with the man in the green plaid shirt. Denny.

As I approached, I could clearly see, Denny had Katy pinned between himself and the wall. I couldn't read her expression. Was there some kind of teen romance going on here? How old was he anyway? I strode right toward them. As I got closer, it was clear Katy was more than uncomfortable. She was scared.

"What's going on?" I said.

Denny didn't move, simply looked over his shoulder at me. "None of your business."

I stepped closer and realized where I'd seen him. "You were at the bar Wednesday night. You're an adult, and she's only fifteen. That makes it my business, buddy."

He slowly turned to face me. "We ain't doin' nothing wrong."

Cocky SOB. "She isn't. You are. Now step away."

"What are you jealous?" He grinned the grin of an arrogant bastard. He reached out and slapped me on the butt.

It took me by surprise, but I reacted, chopping his wrist with my hand as he pulled it away.

He rubbed his wrist with his other hand and glared menacingly at me. "Who the hell do you think you are?"

"I'm the woman who's going to make your life a living hell if you touch me like that again, or you even think of coming near this girl again."

His face started to turn red. Obviously, he wasn't used to being talked to like that. Especially by a woman.

Good.

He stepped closer to me and propped his hands on his hips. "What did you say to me?"

I didn't back down. "I said to step away. And don't come

back."

He huffed. "Piss off."

"I don't think so, creep." I stepped toward Katy, putting myself between them. "Go on, Katy," I said.

He shook his head. "She ain't goin' nowhere, bitch."

His hand came up to shove me. I caught him at the elbow, bent it back, twisted up, and knocked him off balance, slamming him into the wall.

Enraged, he lunged at me. I sidestepped, catching his elbow again, swinging it up so he'd go down. I bent my knee, just so, so he'd catch it with his eye on the way down, and as he fell, I let my hand slide along his arm to his wrist. Pinning him with a thumb lock and my hand on the back of his arm, I kept his face in the hay as he moaned.

"Like I said, I don't think so." I looked up at Katy. She stood, staring at me with her mouth hanging open. "Go on back to your mom," I told her. "He won't bother you again." I kicked him in the side. "Will you?"

"Screw you."

"Apparently, he needs a little more encouragement." I kicked him again.

"Bitch."

I stepped on his thigh and, keeping my hold on his thumb, leaned down to whisper in his ear. "Would you prefer I rip your arm out at the shoulder socket to get the answer I want?"

He shook his head.

Katy took off.

"So, I've made myself clear?"

He nodded. *Pathetic.* Were all these cowboys bull-headed and loaded with testosterone?

I dropped his arm and left him where he lay. As I walked away, I stepped on his hat, partly because I could and partly to emphasize my point.

Then I saw her. The woman, Raina. She'd seen everything.

As I walked by her, she quietly said, "You're no journalist."

I stopped in my tracks. *Crap. Did I just blow my cover?*

"I just know how to defend myself."

"Where'd you learn that?"

I shrugged like it was no big deal. "Sometimes I end up asking questions people aren't keen on answering." This was absolutely true.

"You find yourself in trouble a lot?"

"Not that often," I lied.

Raina stared, looking me up and down. She wasn't convinced.

CHAPTER 10

Crap. She knows. She knows I'm not a journalist. Does she suspect I'm law enforcement? Dammit!

I had to get this under control. There was no way she was Julie's aunt. Something didn't add up there. But who was she? And what would she do with her suspicions?

She said she stayed in her van. A motorhome? I'd seen one when I arrived, the first day, parked outside the diner. It had to be hers and she probably had it parked somewhere on the expo grounds.

I walked the parking area until I found it and discreetly snapped a picture of her license plate. Then I headed back to my car to call Greg.

He answered on the first ring. "How's the bull riding going?"

"Hey, I need you to—what? How'd you know about that?"

He laughed. "A guess. But now you totally have to give it up. You rode a bull?"

"No. Just a mechanical bull. It was—I had to. I was working undercover and—never mind."

"Never mind? Are you kidding? I'm stuck at a computer all day. Give it up."

"There's nothing to tell. I got roped into riding it at the bar Wednesday night."

"Roped into it, huh? Nice play on words."

"Can we just get to what I need please?"

"Sure, cowgirl."

"Don't call me that."

"Whatever. You're in a mood."

"Yeah, I just had to intervene—I may have—would you please run a plate for me?"

"Sure thing," he said, his tone of voice changed to a professional one.

"Thanks." I gave him the state and numbers.

"Give me a second."

I bit my lip. Here I was, in charge of this operation, finally, my own op, and I'd probably already blown my cover. *Ugh.*

"Nothing's coming up."

"Nothing? What do you mean, nothing?"

"You got a last name for her?"

"No. Raina was all I got."

"Can't find anyone by that name in that state, no matter how you spell it. Nothing comes up. The van plate is registered to a company. I bet it's a shell corporation."

"I need you to find out."

"Okay."

"I also need info on Dennis Johnson. He's Julie's neighbor. Dog breeder."

I waited, chewing on a fingernail. Bad habit, I know.

"He pops up. He has a sealed file. Probably something from when he was a minor."

That was no surprise. "Get it unsealed."

"But I can't do that without—"

"I know you can."

Silence. Finally, Greg said, "So, is the journalist cover not working out so swell? I mean, I kinda thought it was an odd choice if your goal is to stay under the radar. Aren't journalists known for being annoying?"

I rolled my eyes. Now he tells me. "Why didn't you mention this before?"

"You cut me off."

"I, what—don't even."

"Maybe you can turn it around."

"How?"

"If you ask me, a good journalist pokes the bear."

"Fine. Fair point. The ranchers won't talk to me anyway. Maybe that's what I should do."

"Yeah," he said, with way too much enthusiasm.

But first I had to figure out who this Raina was and what she knew.

I stopped by my room at Gladys's place, took a shower and a big, deep breath. I could handle this. What did Raina really know? Nothing. Just because I stepped in, lost my temper a little, showed I had some martial art skills, didn't mean I wasn't a journalist. It didn't mean anything at all.

She was the one whose story didn't jive. Julie's aunt. From the city. Who just happened to have sophisticated thermal-imaging security equipment. Yeah, that didn't add up. I needed to find out exactly what her story was.

After I scarfed down a cheese sandwich, courtesy of Gladys, I headed for the honky-tonk. Casey would be good cover to keep an eye out for Raina. She'd been there on Wednesday, maybe she'd be there again.

The parking lot was packed to the gills. Trucks were parked alongside the road for a quarter mile in either direction. But Raina's van stood out, a shiny new Mercedes motorhome. I managed to tuck my rental into a corner of the lot across from her van. I tried to peek in the windows, but the blinds were shut tight.

Entering the building was like stepping into a country-western movie. Casey was right, this looked like the party of the year. Everyone of drinking age from the entire county and beyond was here, line dancing or drinking or both.

I scanned the place for Raina and found her at the bar with an older man, late fifties, maybe sixties, clean shaven, dressed the same as every other cowboy in the place. I had seen her here with him before.

About eight bar stools to her left, Casey leaned on the bar, his eyes on me. Had he been watching for me to arrive?

I headed toward him. "There you are."

"I'm glad you came." He held up his hand to get the attention of the bartender. "Sierra Nevada again?"

"Sure, thanks." Even though he was inches away, I had to yell over the music and ruckus of the crowd. "You been here long?"

"Nope. Had to stay for the bull riding, of course. Didn't see you there."

"Yeah, well, I'm ready to compete with the big boys, for sure, but I figured my ego needed a couple more days to heal."

He grinned. "It just takes practice."

Over his shoulder, I saw Raina stand up and slam back a shot.

"Did you enjoy the stock show?" he asked.

"It was interesting."

"Did you learn anything about what we talked about? The culture?"

"A little. I was hoping you and I could talk some more."

He smiled.

"But it's so loud in here."

"Yeah. It's a party, that's for sure."

Raina staggered backward. *How long had* she *been here?*

The bartender handed Casey my beer, in a bottle. "Sorry. We blew the keg."

"No problem," I said, flattered he'd remembered me.

Casey passed the bottle to me. I took a sip. Ice cold. I relaxed a little.

"So how long do you think you'll be in town?" Casey asked.

"I don't know. At least a couple weeks."

"Long enough for you to find time to go to dinner with me?"

I smiled. "Maybe." *What would Dalton think? Doesn't matter. This is part of the job and Dalton hasn't bothered showing up yet.*

"You like to play hard to get, don't you?"

"I like to keep my options open." I had meant for it to sound flirty but with Dalton on my mind it came out a little short instead. I realized it wasn't exactly the message I wanted to send. Casey liked me and I wanted information from him. Planning a date was to my advantage. "I didn't mean it like that. I just meant, you know, my schedule. I have to get my story while I'm here. No one else is paying my rent."

He seemed to accept my explanation.

I took a swig of my beer. "You line dance?" I asked, pointing toward the dance floor.

"Nah. You?"

"Nah."

We watched for a while as the dancers hopped and twirled in unison to a Billy Ray Cyrus tune. I took another drink and tried to push Dalton from my mind. *Achy breaky heart indeed.* He and I had danced on our first op together. He'd surprised me, taking me by the hand and leading me around the dance floor like a pro. Dancing with him had felt right, natural. Chris was right, I needed to tell him how I felt about him. *If he ever comes back.*

Raina stumbled by, toward the restroom. A few minutes later, she tottered back and ordered more shots. She hadn't even seemed to notice me.

Raina seemed to really be tying one on. She didn't seem concerned about her own safety, way out here in the middle of nowhere. Yet she had seemed worried about Julie and Katy. Was it because of Denny, the neighbor? Is that why she'd been in the kennel area too? Checking on Katy? Maybe this wasn't the first run-in with him.

But why would she point the camera at the barn?

"I do like the slow dances though," Casey broke into my thoughts. I turned my attention back to him and smiled but it was too loud, and I was too distracted for us to continue a conversation. The noise was actually a good cover for my wandering mind.

I watched the crowd for a while longer and decided that trying to get any information out of Casey tonight would be futile. Relationship building was part of my job and I was going to try to kick back and enjoy the evening. I might even take him up on that slow dance. I looked back into his crystal blue eyes. Then I noticed movement over his shoulder.

Raina set an empty glass on the bar and rooted around in her purse for some cash. Was she leaving?

Change of plans. "You know, this has been a long day," I told Casey. "I'm really beat. I think I'm going to turn in."

Raina slapped the cash on the bar next to the glass and kissed the man she was with on the cheek. She was definitely leaving.

"Are you sure? It's early yet," Casey said.

"Yeah, yeah." I handed him the half-full bottle. "Thanks for the beer. I'll have to catch up with you later. For that dinner. I promise."

That made him smile. "I'll hold you to it."

"I hope you do." I rushed to the exit. I wanted to be ahead of her so she didn't think I was following her.

I got to my car and was in the driver's seat before I saw her come out the door. I figured she'd stumble around a bit, wondering where she'd parked. But she stood up straight and walked right to the truck parked next to her van, looked around the lot before crouching down between the vehicles.

What was she doing?

I watched. The bed on the passenger side of the truck started to lower. She was letting the air out of the tire.

She wasn't drunk. And she wanted whomever owned that truck to be delayed. Was it the man she'd been with? That was the most plausible person. They probably arrived together, parked next to each other, and went in.

She got into her van, fired it up, and pulled out of the parking lot. I couldn't follow. She'd notice for sure, since she was obviously stone-cold sober.

I dialed Greg.

"It's Saturday night," he said by way of an answer.

"I need you to run a plate."

"I'm at home."

"Yeah? So? I know you can do it."

"Whatever. Hold on." I heard the crinkling of a potato chip bag and the meow of a cat being shoved from his lap. *Greg has a cat?*

"I did find out about the plate from earlier, by the way," he said over the sound of his computer firing up. "Definitely a shell corporation, which is odd. All I can say is, she's probably not who she says she is."

Tell me something I don't know. "Anything on Bobby and Bart?"

"There's no one officially employed at the Split Fork ranch by those names. They're probably working cash under the table. If you can get me their last names, I could get more."

"What about Denny's record?"

"Still working on it. Give me a break. It's the weekend."

"What? I'm working."

"Yeah, well, some of us have a life you know."

"Did I interrupt a date? Put her on the phone. I'll make the apologies and—"

"Never mind. What's the plate number?"

I gave it to him. Two minutes later he had the info. "Emmett Johnson."

"Johnson? Is the address next to New Hope Farm?"

"It sure is."

"Thanks," I said and put my car in gear. "One more thing. Can you check on a family connection? As in, does Julie have an aunt named Raina?"

"Hold on."

I drove out of the lot and onto the main road. The Johnson farm was about fifteen miles away.

"I can't find one," Greg finally said. "Not a biological aunt, anyway. I'll keep looking."

"Okay, thanks. And hey, sorry to interrupt your Saturday night. Give your cat a kiss for me."

As I came around the curve in the road, I killed my headlights and coasted by the farm. Raina's van was in the driveway. Bold. But she probably had a backup story all prepared if he came back before she expected.

I parked my car alongside the road, far enough to be out of view, and ran through the dark, across the corner of Julie's property and into the yard of the Johnson home.

The house was huge—the kind of ranch home where three generations could live together comfortably.

Not one light was on in the house, but I caught sight of a flashlight, moving around in a front room. A home office? I sneaked up to the window and peered in. Raina was methodically going through some paperwork, snapping photos with her camera as she went.

What is she up to?

This definitely wasn't about Denny hitting on her fifteen-year-old niece. If she was even Julie's aunt, which I doubted highly at this point.

Whatever she was doing, I wasn't going in there to find out. I needed to learn more about her.

I circled back to the driveway and around to the door of her motorhome. With my hand on the edge of the door, I gave the latch a gentle tug. It was locked. Of course, why would she have unlocked this door.

I crept around to the driver's door. The handle moved when I took hold of it, but if I opened the door, the dome light would come on. What were the odds she'd see? Didn't matter, this was probably my only chance. I flung the door open, got inside, pulled it closed behind me, and held my hand over the dome light until it went out while I stared at the Johnson's back door.

She didn't see me. At least she didn't come barging out the door. I probably had five minutes at most, though. I flicked on the flashlight on my phone. *Where do I start?*

The motorhome was plush, with leather seats and that fresh-from-the-factory smell. The glovebox seemed the most likely spot to find some documents. I sat down in the passenger seat and popped it open. Nothing. Empty.

Okay. The kitchen cabinets were stuffed with dishes and food. The cabinets over the dinette had more food. I moved into the bedroom in the back. Clothes, shoes, coats. All items any vacationer would have. I lifted the mattress. The box under the bed was solid. Maybe there was storage access there from outside?

The little bathroom had nothing out of the ordinary.

Now what? Everyone had a laptop. Was it locked up somewhere?

Above the cab was a full-sized bunk. Was there storage up there? Behind the passenger seat was a step to get up into the bunk. Did I have time? I took a hold of the handle, put my foot on the step, lifted myself to look, and the driver's side door flung open. The dome light came on.

I sprang onto the bunk and froze. *Did she see me? Did she hear me?*

The door slammed shut. A key slid into the ignition and the engine fired up. I let out my breath. She shifted into reverse and the motorhome started to move.

Crap. Wherever we were headed, I was on my own. I had no

idea who this woman was or what she was capable of. Maybe I could get away with hiding in the bunk, sneak out later without her ever knowing, but I wasn't sure it was going to gain me anything. I was tempted to check the storage cabinets while I was up here, but surely she'd hear me. I wasn't ready to reveal my presence. I wanted to know where she was headed next.

The sound of a phone being dialed came over the speakers. She was calling someone. After three rings, the person answered.

"Yo."

Omigod. The guy reminded me of Greg.

"Sorry to bother you so late. I just sent you some files while I had wireless access. Tell me they got there because I was running out of time."

She had a partner, or tech support like Greg. Was she law enforcement?

"Yep, got 'em right here."

"Good. The phone service out here sucks."

Tell me about it.

"I'll get back with you in the morning."

"Yep."

The call was disconnected.

So, Raina wasn't working alone. On whatever it was she was doing.

The motorhome slowed and she made a left turn onto a gravel road, the road that ran along the south side of Julie's property. We didn't get far and she slowed and made another left. The motorhome bumped along on a rutted drive, then slowed and came to a stop.

Was this where she stayed for the night? Was that part of her story true? She parked on the corner of Julie's property?

Raina put it in park and killed the engine. My heart rate shot up. I had to decide what to do. Hide or confront her? If I even had the choice. She might discover me on her own. I doubted she had a weapon on her. That would be hard to explain if Mr.

Johnson had come home before she got out of the house.

She got up from the seat and moved through the dark into the motorhome. There was a click and the interior lights came on. Her back was to me.

I slid down from the bunk, purposefully slamming my feet on the floor with a loud thump.

She spun around. "What the hell?" Her hands came up in a defensive posture, her body poised to fight. She was trained.

My reflexes kicked in. My hands were up. My feet shifted into an aggressive posture.

CHAPTER 11

Her eyes gave her away as she sized-me up. She'd seen me slam Denny to the ground. She knew I had skills.

"What the hell are you doing in my motorhome?"

I slowly lowered my hands, showing her I didn't want a fight. "I was poking around. Just like you." I paused. Her expression didn't change. She kept her hands out front, at the ready. "Some would call that breaking and entering."

"You a cop?"

"Do I look like a cop?"

She sighed. "It's not what you think."

"Really? What do I think?"

She relaxed a little. "Okay, that I don't know."

"I know you let the air out of Emmett Johnson's tire."

"Yeah, well." She started to lower her hands. "I'm telling you. It's not what you think." She made no move to threaten me. At least that was a good sign.

"So, enlighten me. Or I'll tell Mr. Johnson what you've been up to."

"Believe me, it wouldn't serve the cause." She was starting to look very uncomfortable. Not panicking, but her voice was strained.

"The cause?"

"Let's just say I'm the good guy here."

Something about her demeanor made me believe her. Her

behavior—the poking around, the video—all pointed to her trying to get information, not perpetrate a crime.

"Okay, I believe you. But still."

Raina sighed and dropped her hands to her sides. "Might as well have this discussion over a cup of tea."

I gave her a shrug and moved to the little couch, keeping a close eye on her as she poured water into a kettle from a jug, and set it to boil on the tiny stovetop.

Raina set two mugs on the counter, placed a tea bag in each, then sat down on the couch next to me. "I'm an investigative journalist."

I'd made a quick assessment. The cabinets in the kitchenette were made of real wood, not that pressed board they put in cheap motorhomes. The faucet in the sink shined. This little home on wheels had cost a fortune. Not exactly something a journalist was likely to afford.

I looked at her skeptically.

"I know. Big coincidence, huh?"

Nope. Didn't believe her. It didn't quite add up. But I decided to play along. "What are you investigating?"

"Land disputes."

"What kind of land disputes?"

Raina hesitated and looked pointedly at me, trying to read my face. "How do I know I can trust you?"

"Did I call the cops on you for breaking and entering?"

She grinned and relaxed a degree. "Good point." But then her face became serious once more. "You're not a journalist. Obviously, I would know."

"I am." I frowned. "Apparently just not a very good one. I'm starting to see how an undercover approach would have been a better option, probably get me a lot more information."

She nodded, seeming to accept my explanation. Or pretending to. We were both testing, trying not to reveal too much. "They don't like outsiders around here. Especially nosey ones. It's taken me some time to get close."

"Close to whom?"

"Emmett Johnson. It helped that he's a lonely old widower. Though I have to deal with the bad breath and that slow drawl." She rolled her eyes.

"Why Emmett Johnson?"

The teakettle whistled. She rose from the couch, poured hot water into our mugs, then handed me mine. She tucked one leg under her as she sat back down on the couch. "The Johnson boys haven't exactly been good neighbors."

"Why don't you just tell me what's going on instead of beating around the bush?"

She looked annoyed. "Because it's *my* story."

I waved my hand, dismissing my question. "No worries. We've all got stories. I'm not going to steal yours. But maybe we can help each other. How about that?"

She thought for a moment, then nodded. "All right. Tell me yours."

"I haven't been hiding it. I'm here to find out what's happening with the wolves and the increase in livestock depredation. Pretty simple."

"Yeah, and what was that back in the kennels today? With Denny?"

"Simple. I saw an adult getting sexually aggressive with a young girl. I lost my temper. Sounds like you're not liking Denny Johnson very much either."

"No, not at all. The apple doesn't fall far from the tree."

"So, I told you mine. What's this land issue?"

She took a sip of her tea. "The Johnson farm has been in that family for generations. It's one of the largest in the area. A few generations back, Ida Johnson, just nineteen at the time, got pregnant, out of wedlock. She refused to reveal the identity of the father. Well, as you can imagine, that didn't go over well. Mr. Johnson wanted to kick her out, send her off to the city, whatever, who knows, but disown her nonetheless. His wife fought against it. She wouldn't abandon her daughter. An old ranch hand had a little shack in the corner of the property, on what is now Julie's land. He'd passed away and Mr. Johnson agreed to let his daughter live there, as long as she was out of sight."

This kind of story, so typical of that era, made me want to scream.

"Ida was resourceful. She planted a garden, acquired some chickens. She really made a life for herself and her son. The kid grew up and left for the city. Lo and behold, the young man comes back years later with a law degree. When the old man died, his illegitimate grandson made a claim on the land. Some kind of squatters rights or something, I don't know. Doesn't matter, because the grandmother, then in her eighties, didn't fight it. She signed off on it. That young man was Julie's grandfather."

"So, the dispute is about the ownership transfer all those years ago?"

She shook her head. "No. Emmett tried that at first but found out it's rock solid. He's offered to buy it over the years. Julie's grandma wouldn't sell."

"And I assume Julie won't either."

She nodded.

"So, where's the story? Why does he even care about 640 acres, anyway? He's got thousands."

"Julie told me you rode out with Jack the other day, up into the hills."

"Yeah."

"You crossed the river."

"Yeah."

"It's the only shallow spot in that river for miles in either direction."

"Okay." I wasn't following.

"It's the way of life out here. Cattle and sheep farmers rely on acres and acres of public lands for grazing. They move their animals all season. Especially sheep farmers, from the valleys in the spring, up into the higher elevations throughout the summer."

I was starting to understand. "And that part of the river is the only place to cross into the hills, directly onto the public land."

"Bingo," she said, punctuating in the air with her finger. "Right now, Emmett has to truck his livestock to public lands. Do you know how expensive that is?"

"I can imagine."

"When there's a path right next door. On land that *used* be his. At least that's how he sees it. As his birthright."

I took a sip of my tea, taking the moment to digest what she was telling me. "Julie's land must be worth a small fortune, then. Did she consider selling it to him?"

She shook her head. "Doesn't matter. She can't. The land is technically owned by a trust with certain use restrictions."

"Maybe she could charge a fee, let him move the sheep across in the spring."

"Do you know how much damage sheep do? Not an option. This is Julie's dream. She can't sell the land and buy somewhere else. It's here or nowhere."

"So, what were you doing in his house?"

She leaned back, eyed me again. "Yeah, I was crossing a line there. Trying to see if he was in financial trouble or something."

She was lying. Or at least not telling me the full truth. "All part of the story." I took another sip of my tea. "Do you think Denny poisoned Sannyu?"

She shook her head, frowned. "I don't know."

"Julie has had some bad luck lately. A bad neighbor, Sannyu getting poisoned, and the wolves attacking her chickens. Seems like an awful lot of coincidences." I watched her closely for her reaction to my next question. "Julie showed me the video of the wolves." She didn't flinch. "She said you were worried about their safety. But that's some expensive equipment you're using. High tech for a journalist."

"Yeah, well, I'm well-funded."

That didn't quite add up either. But I let it go for now. "Why surveil the barn?"

She gave me a half shrug. "Those chickens were the only thing she has of value."

I sat back. "Someone's poisoning the wolves. Not a surprise. Won't make the front page. But it's illegal, nonetheless. And I plan to find out who."

"Admirable," she said. "I have an idea." Her eyes held a hint of mischief.

"Lay it on me," I said, looking at her expectantly.

"We can work together, like you said. I can pay closer attention, help you find out who might be behind the poisoning. You can help me find out more about the Johnsons."

"Okay. What do you have in mind?"

"You've already revealed that you're a journalist. Maybe we can use that to our advantage. Put on the pressure. See who blows."

"You want me to poke the bear."

"If you're willing. We can play a good cop/bad cop thing."

Ah, the irony. "That could work." What did I have to lose? If she was willing to give me information, I'd take it.

"I'm supposed to meet Emmett at the diner for breakfast at nine tomorrow morning."

"I'll be there."

I opted to walk back to my car. It wasn't quite a mile and there was a bright half-moon to light my way. The night air was refreshing, and I needed the time to think.

Raina wasn't telling me everything. That much was clear. But that didn't mean she wasn't trustworthy. If she knew more of the story, there was no reason to give it up to me, a potential rival. I hoped that was all it was. If she could get the information I wanted, it would be worth working with her.

A sound came from the hills that brought me to a halt. Howls. One voice, then a second. Nothing compares to the haunting call of wolves. It could make the hair on the back of your neck stand up. If you feared them, I guess. To me, it was music, a harmony like no other. It was the song of nature, of all that gave balance to the world. It was primal, and spoke to something inside me, something that grounded me, made me feel whole.

The howl ended abruptly, and I waited but didn't hear it again, so I continued on, disappointed.

It had been a long day. I thought of the two men who had stood in that booth today, all fired up and excited to invite me to a wolf derby. *There's a prize for the hunter who kills the biggest wolf.* Why? They weren't hunting for meat, to put food on the table. They weren't hunting to protect their loved ones. They were killing for the sake of killing. Glorifying the so-called hunt. They could come up with all the reasons they wanted; none were based in real science. Myths born out of fear and anger. That side of human nature was so frustrating.

This whole case was frustrating. A mess. A political mess based in misinformation and ignorance. Everyone out here hated wolves for one reason or another. Everyone. How could I change their minds?

When I got back to the car, I had two messages on my phone. The first was from Mike.

"I'm here. Got the job. You happy? Thanks for nothing."

Oh, there's a surprise; Mike wasn't happy with me.

The second message was from Tom. "I just got in. Got a room twenty-five miles out at a roadside motel for the night. Give me a call. How do you want to go about this?"

At least somebody was being professional about their job. I called him back right away.

"Hey, Poppy. How's it going?"

"It's going."

"That bad, huh?"

"Have you heard from Dalton?"

"No. Why would I? He's on vacation, isn't he?"

"Oh yeah. Right."

"You okay?"

"I'm just…this whole situation is complicated."

"Yeah, I know. I've been reading about the history of wolves and the politics surrounding it all. It's complicated, that's for sure."

"Politics and ignorance."

"Poppy."

"Yeah?"

"You're doing fine. Hyland put you in a charge for a reason. You're a good agent. You've got good instincts."

I sighed. "Thanks Tom. I've got to meet someone in the morning, follow up on a lead, then we'll meet, and I'll fill you in."

"Sounds good."

The diner was packed, a line out the door. I squeezed through, hoping to find a single stool at the counter.

Right away, I saw Raina sitting in a booth with Emmett at her side. The seat across from them was empty.

As I passed by, turning to look at the other side of the room, I came face to face with Denny. He must have been coming from the restroom. He took hold of my arm and leaned into my ear. "You're a long way from home, little girl. Meddling in things you don't know nothing about. You're gonna get hurt."

I turned to face him. "How's that eye feeling?"

Next to me, his father, Emmett, rose from the booth. "What's the trouble?"

"Nuttin'," Denny muttered.

"Yeah, well sit your ass down," he said.

Raina poked her head around Emmett's waist. "There's

not another empty seat in the place. Why don't you join us, dear?"

Denny huffed.

Emmet frowned at him. "Yes, young lady. Why don't you join us?" He held out his hand, gesturing for me to sit next to Denny. *Great.*

I plopped down in the seat.

"Coffee?" Emmett offered. I nodded. He turned over the empty mug at my place setting and filled it from a thermal pot. "What brings you to Elk Valley?" He spoke in a slow, direct voice, as though he were a man who didn't speak much, but when he did, it was deliberate.

"You haven't heard yet?" I said. "I'm surprised. It seems word gets around fast in this town." *Except I bet Denny here didn't tell you that I'm the one who gave him that shiner.*

He seemed amused. "You're right. I was being polite. I've *heard* that you're writing a story about the wolf killings, though I don't know why. It's nothing new."

"I'm more interested in the bigger picture, how and why wolves and men can't seem to get along." If I was going to poke, might as well poke hard.

The corner of his mouth slowly rose in the hint of a smirk as he wrapped his hand around his coffee cup. He had the hands of a rancher, strong and weathered. "Well, it's obvious, isn't it? We want the same things and we can't both get what we want."

A family got up from a table across the room, and before the waitress could get there to clean it off, a crew of cowboys headed for it. Mike was with them, walking bowlegged, obviously uncomfortable from horse riding the day before. I felt a smirk sneak onto my face and quickly wiped it away.

He gave me a shrug, a signal that he had no information to share yet. Bobby and Bart weren't in the group.

I turned back to Emmett. "I don't know if I agree with you. I mean, the reason wolves go after livestock is because they're easy pickings. But generally, they seem to do just fine hunting elk and deer, their natural prey."

"But they don't, for the exact reason you cite. My sheep make for an easy meal. My calves, too. And I don't take too kindly to it."

Raina was nodding emphatically, making sure Emmett knew she was on his side.

"But to be fair," I said, "isn't it true that according to a recent Department of Agriculture report, way more cattle die due to disease and weather issues than wolves. In fact, only point two percent die from carnivore depredation. That's two out of a thousand."

"That's two more than I want to lose."

"But, is killing them for it the only answer?"

He shrugged. He didn't care one way or the other. He was calm as could be. I was supposed to be getting him riled up.

"It's simple," he said. "When wolves mind their own business, I got no problem with them. But when wolves kill livestock, they got to go. And don't look at me with that long face. It's the policy of the U.S. government and who am I to question it?"

It was true. Frustratingly true. "Don't you think that's a little unfair? When you take your livestock onto public lands, it seems to me it's setting up the wolves to fail right from the get-go. Like setting bait for them."

"I'm not sure what you mean. My sheep have just as much right to be out there as any wolf does. I got all the proper permits and I pay my fees." He still wasn't getting heated. He had his views and he was sharing them, his eyes full of flinty intelligence. He took another sip of his coffee. "Let me guess, you're going to ask me about bears and mountain lions next, aren't you?"

"Okay, sure. What about bears and mountain lions?"

"They mind their own business. Sure, every once in a while, one of them gets one of mine. But a mountain lion? Sheep never see him coming. Wolves, they cost me big."

"How do you mean?"

"It's the way they hunt. They harass my flocks, sometimes for days, putting them constantly on alert. My cattle don't graze all day like they should. They got their heads up, watching. Sheep, too. Then when they do attack, they run 'em, separate the herds, burn their precious calories."

The waitress finally stopped by, set another coffee pot on the table, and yanked a pad from her apron. "What can I getcha?"

"Two eggs scrambled."

"That it?"

"Yes, thank you."

She shook her head as she walked away.

"I'm not saying we should eradicate all the wolves. They got their place. But they need to be controlled. There's a problem wolf, it needs to go."

I suddenly realized why this man wasn't fired up, like the young cowboys I'd met a few weeks ago. Arrogance. He thought he was above all the petty bickering. His view was supported by the government, by the local culture. It was in no danger of being challenged, at least not in any way that mattered to him. A young journalist, miles from home, out of her element, was an amusement to him.

I had to plow on. "Do you understand how killing a problem wolf, as you call them, usually makes depredation worse?"

Denny smirked. Emmett threw him a dirty look.

"I bet you're going to enlighten me," Emmett said.

"When someone takes it into their own hands, let's say shoots a wolf they catch killing their stock, the odds are it's an alpha. That's a pack leader."

"I know what an alpha is."

I bet you do. "With an alpha gone, the pack splinters, and by the next year, the remaining wolves have formed their own packs. Now there's more than one pack in a territory, led by less experienced hunters, and they have to spread out. See where I'm going with this?"

He sat back. "Maybe you're right. Maybe we should just eradicate them all."

I frowned. "Sir, do you feel any moral obligation to wildlife?"

His bottom lip came up as though he was considering my question. "No. I believe in survival of the fittest."

"What about what the Bible says?" Now I was really stretching. I'm not a religious person, but I was pulling out all the stops.

He crossed his arms, looked me right in the eyes. "Are you referring to Genesis chapter one, verse twenty-six: And God said, let us make man in our image, according to our likeness; and let them have dominion over the fish of the sea and over the birds of heaven and over the cattle and over all the earth and over every creeping thing that creeps upon the earth."

My mouth stuck open for a moment. Who does that? Whips out any old bible verse from memory? "Yes, that's the one. Some people interpret that to mean we have a responsibility to care for nature in a way that's consistent with God's will."

He held my gaze. "Do you think that's what dominion means?"

"Maybe. Maybe not. But I do know that if humankind doesn't care for the animals of this Earth, they'll be gone, and we'll regret it. Because soon afterward, we'll be gone."

He held up a finger. "That's the smartest thing you've said yet."

"Thank you?"

"What is it you want from me?"

"Well, we were just having a conversation, but now that you ask, would you consider other methods to deal with your so-called wolf problem? Non-lethal methods?"

"Now I *know* you're a wolf-lover," he smirked as he sat back, still game. "Sounds expensive. And time-consuming."

"It doesn't have to be. All I'm asking is, would you be

willing to consider it?"

"For you, little lady, sure."

Denny huffed beside me.

I couldn't tell if he was bored with me now and thought that'd be the end of it or what. He wasn't getting off that easily. "The techniques have been working for some ranchers in south Idaho. I'm sure they'll work here, too. In fact, a representative from that group is here in town. I'm sure he'd like to talk to you."

Emmett shook his head.

"You just said—"

"I tell you what, he can talk to Hector. You can go, too. Whatever suits your fancy. Hector's my sheepherder. If you want to head up into the hills, find him and convince him to give it a try, you got my blessing."

CHAPTER 12

Tom and I chose a crossroads halfway between us to meet. As I drove in that direction, I called Greg. I needed him to dig around some more, see if he could verify Raina's story about the Johnson land deed.

"It's Sunday morning," he said, sounding groggy when he picked up.

"Yep. Did you not realize this job is a twenty-four seven thing?"

"It wasn't until I got assigned to you. I don't think I like being your call-boy."

"Um…right."

There was an awkward silence. "You know that's not what I meant, right?"

"I need you to look into some land deeds." I gave him the details.

"Done."

"And has Emmett Johnson ever been arrested on anything?"

"That I can do right now. Hold on."

I pulled over, consulted my county map, then continued on.

"Here he is, Emmett P. Johnson, wife, Louise M. Johnson, deceased, sons Casey and Dennis Johnson. I don't see—"

"Wait. Casey? Could you look, is he the same Casey who owns Elk Valley Lodge? It's a hunting guide service."

I heard the familiar click-click-click of his keyboard. "Yep. Same guy."

Dammit. How'd I miss that? "Where's the lodge?"

"Let me bring up Google maps. Okay, it's on the northeast corner of the Johnson property, borders the public lands."

Of course it is. "Would you check him out, too? Make sure his permits, all that jazz, are up to date, whether he has a clean record, etcetera."

"Consider it done. But hold on. I just got an alert."

"An alert?"

"Yeah, I set up alerts on relevant developments."

"Relevant developments, huh? Now there's a tongue twister."

"Yeah, this twist will get you. I hate to break it to you, but Jack Wade filed a request for the state to issue a control action."

"What are you saying? What's a control action?"

"It's an official state government approval that would give him permission to destroy the whole wolf pack." He muttered as he scanned the document. "He cites the recent killings, lists the complaints from locals, includes the reimbursement files."

"Well, what does that mean? I mean, you're saying this is an interagency thing. He's a federal employee, but this is under state purview, so he has to make a formal request?"

"Yes. Looks that way."

"What happens next? Can they deny it?"

"I assume, because the document he's filed is actually called a request."

"But they won't." *Dammit!* "How long do I have?"

"Could be a couple days, might be a week."

"Can you find out?"

"I can let you know when a document is filed that it's been approved. Other than that—"

"Dammit!"

"I'm sorry, I know you—"

"If Jack gets the approval, that means he will…what? What would he do next?"

"Says here on USDA's Wildlife Services web page that the agency will employ any number of methods including trapping, snaring, shooting, and the use of chemical products and immobilization and euthanasia drugs to remove or kill offending predators."

My stomach roiled.

"Oh, yikes."

"What?"

"It says here—"

"Do I want to know?"

"They sometimes use helicopters to find the pack and gun them down from the air *to expedite elimination of the threat*."

My throat constricted. "Yeah, because poisoning isn't quick enough." The words came out as a croak.

"It's Sunday. Nothing's going to get approved today."

I let out my breath. "Thanks, Greg. Call me the minute you hear otherwise." I disconnected.

I had to figure this out. The wolves were now on death row, with no one fighting for them but me. And I had nothing.

Tom was already at the crossroads when I got there. I pulled up behind him, killed the engine, got out of my car, and got into the passenger side of his.

He looked like he was wearing the same clothes I'd seen him in last in Bimini.

"Wow, you look like you just got news that your grandma died." He winced. "Sorry. That's not it is it?"

"No. I just got news that the whole wolf pack in this area is going to be gunned down if we don't do something."

"Oh," he said, but it sounded a lot like *ouch*. "So, what are we going to do?"

"It's Sunday, so I guess we might as well go on ahead with the plan, go find that sheepherder, Hector, and see if we get anywhere with him. If he agrees, maybe we can call back the posse."

"Okay." There was a long pause. "What sheepherder?"

"Right." I brought him up to speed with what little I knew. "Do you think that's what we should do?"

"I don't know. But you're the one who's been here. You're on point. Whatever you think is good with me."

"Thanks, Tom."

"How do we find him?"

"We'll have to go on horseback." The thought of getting back on a horse made my bottom side ache.

"Okay."

"You know anything about horses?"

"Nope."

Crap.

He stared at me. "But you do, right?"

"Yeah." I'd watched old episodes of *The Lone Ranger* when I was a kid. That counted, right? "I bet we could rent Julie's horses. She could use the cash."

"What are we waiting for then?"

When we pulled into New Hope Farm, Sannyu greeted me with a wagging tail.

"I'm so glad to see you up and around, boy," I said, scratching behind his ears. He looked at Tom with skeptical eyes but didn't bark.

Julie easily agreed to letting us take her horses. I had the sense she didn't feel comfortable about it, but the cash we offered was substantial. I wanted to make it hard to turn down. I had a budget and I was going to use it.

She even offered use of some camping gear—a small tent, sleeping bags, cook stove. "You might not find him right away," she said, "and have to stay out there overnight."

Tom simply shrugged. Another day on the job.

"We'll take that, too, then," I said, and gave her another fifty dollars.

"Tom, you'll ride Henry," she said. "He tends to be calmer with a man."

Tom's eyebrows shot up. "Calmer?"

"He can be finicky."

"Finicky?"

"You know, stubborn."

"Oh, right," Tom said, nodding. It was obvious he had no idea what she meant.

"C'mon, we'll get him saddled first." She led Tom into the barn. I followed. Henry was a creamy cocoa-colored stallion. "He was my grandmother's horse."

Tom seemed to relax. After all, if an elderly woman rode this horse, how finicky could he be?

"I loved my grandmother, but she was a stern old woman. Just keep that in mind," she said, matter of fact.

"I will," Tom said, turning to me where Julie couldn't see, with raised eyebrows.

I shook my head. How was I supposed to know?

"Henry was trained with directional reins, not neck reins."

"Gotcha. Not a problem," Tom said, again, glancing over his shoulder at me, his eyebrows twisted into a question mark.

I smiled, reassuring him all would be well. *Thank God for Google.*

Julie bustled about the barn, getting the horses ready, delivering bits of advice. Once both horses were ready, she snugged the leather straps tight, patted them on the flanks, and said, "Be good to my horses. They're the only ones I've got."

"I promise, we will," I said.

"I have to run Sannyu over to the vet for a follow up. Be careful out there."

We stood in front of the barn, holding our horse's reins, waving goodbye as she rushed to get the dog in the car and head out.

"What luck," I said. "We were going to be in trouble if she

stayed to see us on our way."

"No kidding. What did she mean by directional reins? And all that about him being finicky?" Tom addressed his horse. "Are you finicky?"

I pulled out my phone. "We'll Google it. No problem." I clicked to open my browser app. "Oh crap."

"What?"

"I got no internet service out here."

"You've got to be kidding."

Duchess shifted on her feet and let out a little snort.

"I do have phone service."

Tom glared at me.

"We'll call Greg."

Tom let his head fall back. "Great."

I dialed. He answered. "Yo."

"Yeah, um, Tom and I need a favor."

"Uh-huh."

"We don't have internet service here on the farm and, uh, we need to get going, so, would you please Google how to ride a horse?"

"Are you serious?"

"Serious as a crutch, Rich," I said, trying to lighten the mood.

"What?"

"You never watched *Happy Days*?"

"Are you kidding?"

"Never mind." *Ugh.* "We need to know what directional reins are. As opposed to neck reins. Whatever that means."

"Let me get this straight. You're about to hop on a horse, aren't you? And you want me to give you the Cliff notes version of how to ride it."

"Yeah, pretty much."

"Do you guys take a sanity test for this job?"

"Will you just do it please?"

"All right, all right." I heard the clicking of his keyboard.

Then he stopped. "Hey, how do you know I wasn't in the middle of something?"

"Were you in the middle of something?"

A pause. "No." Click, click, click. "Okay, so." Mutter, mutter, mutter. I put him on speaker. "With directional reining, you actually tug on the rein on the side you want the horse to go. If you're using neck reining, you lay the reins on the neck opposite the side you want the horse to turn. It's more subtle."

Tom nodded that he understood and climbed up onto his horse. He took hold of the reins and gave the left one a tug. Henry responded, turning in a circle. "Cool," Tom said with a grin.

"To go, squeeze the horse with your legs. If you want to stop, pull back on the reins."

"That's it?" Tom asked.

"Yes, Tom, that's horse riding one o' one from Google. Anything else I can help you with? Say, how to tame your tiger?"

"Thanks Greg. We can do this."

"Okay. And by the way, the line is, 'Funny as a crutch, Rich'," he said and hung up.

"He's right about that," Tom said, giving Henry a squeeze. The horse bolted forward and Tom let out a yippee.

I rubbed Duchess on the nose before I climbed into the saddle, more gracefully than the first time, and followed. *I think I'm getting the hang of this. No problem.*

When we reached the river, we stopped to let the horses get a drink. They didn't seem to want to linger, so we moved along.

We didn't talk much. Tom and I both needed to concentrate on how to direct our horses. Considering the circumstances, all was going well. We rode up the hillside, across a higher meadow and into the forest.

Emmett had given me a general area where Hector and the flock were most likely to be. But four hours into the trek, we hadn't seen any signs of them and decided to get off the horses and stretch.

Tom hobbled over to a tree to pee while I held the reins, then I took my turn.

"When we find him, we're going to explain the benefits," I said.

Tom nodded.

"We'll tell him about the success stories."

Tom nodded some more.

"He'll agree."

Tom shrugged.

"You're not feeling optimistic?"

"It's not that. I have nothing to go on. We have no idea what this guy's experience is, what his views are, how he'll respond. His name is Hector, so the odds are he's one of the seasonal sheepherders from Peru who work in this area. He's already doing a tough job. I think the key is to convince him it will make his life easier."

"I'm sure you're right. You should do the talking."

"Me?"

"You're better at diplomacy." I climbed back atop Duchess.

"Am I?"

"Definitely." *Know thyself. And how to use the tools you have. Isn't that what Jesse had told me?*

We trudged on.

By late afternoon, there was still no sign of Hector and the sheep.

We'd found a nice mountain meadow, perfect for grazing, but he was nowhere in sight.

"I'm starting to feel like there's way more ground to cover than we thought," Tom said.

"Yeah. That's exactly what I was feeling."

From the woods that ran along the ridge came the rumble of ATVs.

"Maybe we'll get lucky and someone can give us directions," Tom said.

One ATV appeared, then another, then another, their drivers clad in jeans and Carhartt coats, their faces hidden under their helmets. They raced toward us, full speed, their engines screaming as they bounced over the terrain.

"They're going kinda fast," Tom said.

Duchess sidestepped, then stumbled. She didn't like it. "It's all right, girl," I soothed.

The ATVs kept coming in our direction, hell-bent it seemed.

Tom's horse started to falter. He didn't like those loud machines one bit.

"What the hell?" I said. "They've got miles and miles of mountain trails out here. Why do they have to race through this meadow? Don't they see us?"

Then I had my answer. The lead ATV closed in. The driver made no attempt to slow. He revved his engine and purposefully cut close, making the horses rear back. The second and third followed as the first turned to circle us.

Oh crap.

Around us they zoomed, yipping and hollering like banshees.

Duchess started to panic. She shifted on her feet, not knowing which way to bolt. I pulled back on the reins. "Easy girl. Easy."

Tom was having a harder time keeping Henry calm. The horse threw his head back and lifted his front legs. "Whoa! Whoa!" Tom shouted, tugging on the reins.

The lead ATV driver slammed on his brakes. I turned to see what he was up to. From a pocket, he quickly took something and in his other hand he flicked a lighter.

Oh shit!

He threw something at us. *Boom, kaboom, boom, boom.* Firecrackers. Puffs of smoke appeared around us and the odor of sulphur hit my nose. Duchess reared up. I reacted without thinking, leaning forward to counter balance, like I was back on the bucking bull. Her front hooves slammed to the ground as she came back down and she bolted, racing through the field. I felt the raw power of her muscle and might and held onto the saddle horn for dear life.

Behind me, more firecrackers went off, crackling and booming. I managed to look back. Tom's horse followed, but it was bucking and kicking like a rodeo star. Poor Tom didn't have a chance. His arms and legs flailed as he was launched into the air. He came down fast and hard.

The ATVs raced away, the riders laughing and shouting, "Go home! You don't belong here!"

Once I got Duchess to slow, I got her turned around and headed back to Tom. He lay on the ground on his back, looking up at the sky.

I dismounted and dropped to my knees beside him. "Are you okay?"

He didn't respond.

"Tom, talk to me. Are you hurt? Are you okay?"

He moaned.

"Do you think anything is broken?"

Images flashed in my mind of Dalton, injured in the deep wilderness of Alaska, blood seeping from his leg. Here, I could run for help. Tom would stay still and I'd race back to the farm and—

"Oh hell," he groaned. "That was embarrassing."

"Are you kidding me?"

He tried to push himself up to a seated position. "I told you I couldn't ride a horse."

"What? Have you hit your head? Look in my eyes."

He looked right at me and grinned. "I'm fine. Just got the wind knocked out of me."

Relief flooded over me. I wanted to smack him then. "Don't scare me like that."

"Scare *you*? I just flew off the back of a horse."

"Actually, to say you flew would imply there was some level…of…um, finesse."

"Yeah, no kidding." He looked off into the woods where the ATVs had disappeared. "What the hell was that all about?"

My eyes followed his gaze. "Welcome to Elk Valley. Apparently, the mere mention of wolves around here gets some people riled up."

His gaze swung around to meet mine. "Well, hell."

CHAPTER 13

Tom said, "We might as well find a place to camp."

I sighed. "I was hoping we'd find Hector and be back before dark."

"I know, but what are we going to do? We're out here now. And I don't think I can get back on that horse right now." He pointed. "How about up on that ridge? Maybe we'll get a good view."

"Sure, whatever."

He started walking. I climbed back atop Duchess and headed to get Henry, who was now grazing at the edge of the forest. At least he hadn't run all the way back to the barn. As I approached, he didn't flinch. He let me take hold of his reins and lead him alongside Duchess.

As we crested the ridge, the sun lay on the edge of the horizon. Tom cautiously approached his horse and untied the sack of gear. I dismounted, untied the gear from Duchess's back, and we both stared at the pile of stuff for a moment. "I'll take care of the horses," I said.

"Yeah, I'll pitch the tent and get a fire going."

With both horses, I managed to get the bridles off easily enough, and the girth loosened. I tied their leads to a branch and poured water into their bucket, setting it where I was sure they could reach.

When I brushed my hands off on my pants and heaved a sigh

of exhaustion, I turned to see Tom had the tent set up and a nice fire going. The stove was lit and a pot on top of it.

"It's a can of chicken noodle soup."

"Is that all we have?" I was a vegetarian.

"It's what Julie gave us. I have a feeling anything would taste good right now."

"Yeah." I didn't have a choice. "But you can have my share of the chunks of chicken."

"Excellent," he said with a grin.

When the soup was warm, he poured it into two mugs and handed me one. I sat down on the ground next to the fire. The sun was down by now and the stars were starting to appear in the twilight sky.

"What a beautiful night," Tom said as he carefully lowered himself to sit next to me.

"You sure you're all right?"

He nodded and slurped a mouthful from the mug.

"Yeah. We're lucky," I said. "I think it's ten degrees warmer than it was last night."

Tom took another slurp. "So, what's our directive, exactly? It's a little unclear to me."

"You and me both. Just like in Bimini. I'm supposed to be quietly investigating Jack, but there seems to be a lot more going on."

Tom shook his head. He didn't like it any more than I did. "I don't like flying blind."

"Especially when it seems that the animals aren't our primary concern. I don't get it. I signed up to be on an animal task force."

Tom nodded in agreement. "Something's obviously going on. Those men were pretty clear they didn't want us out here."

"I'm starting to wonder…"

He waited a moment, giving me time to finish my sentence, but when I didn't, he asked, "Wonder what?"

"Nothing."

"Poppy, you're a good agent. A great agent. Whatever you're thinking, you should trust it."

"Wow, I wish Dalton talked like that."

"Well, sometimes Dalton's right, too. Life's complicated."

"Dalton. No kidding. Complicated." I looked at Tom and he gave me a sympathetic smile. "In case you were wondering, we kinda have a thing. A relationship." I probably shouldn't have told him, but Tom felt like someone I could trust. He was so easy to talk to.

"Yeah, I figured."

"That obvious, huh?"

"Nah. It's just, in this line of work, you learn to read people. And if you two aren't meant for each other, I don't know who is."

"We could get fired for it."

He shrugged. "Only if someone knows."

I nodded.

"You two got in a fight in Bimini? That why he's not here? Why he's taking a break?"

"Sorta. I guess. I don't know." *Might as well tell him.* "I think he went to Africa."

Tom thought a moment. "Should I ask?"

"My dad was killed in Africa. When I was a kid. By poachers."

"I'm sorry to hear that."

"Thanks. I think Dalton went to see what he could find out. Like, maybe he's afraid I'll go on my own someday and I'll make a mess of it."

"I doubt that."

I stared at him. "Doubt that he went to keep me from going? Or that I'd make a mess of it? Because the way you said that, it was unclear, and I'm not sure—"

He smiled. "I doubt Dalton thinks that. He respects you. Sure, you're unorthodox in your approach, but you get things done. It's one of those relationship things marriage counselors talk about, you know, the two-sided coin. The thing you love about someone is the same thing that ends up driving you crazy."

"How do you know so much about it?"

"Relationships? I've had a few."

"I didn't mean—sorry."

He slurped some more of his soup. I fished the chicken chunks out of mine with a spoon and dropped them into his mug.

"Listen," he said, "it's none of my business, but I say go for it. It's hard enough to find someone to love in this world. If you find someone special, screw everything else, including a job."

"You sound like my friend Chris."

"Is he a Buddhist monk?"

I laughed. "No. But close."

"For what it's worth, I don't know if I'm meant for this task force either. I'm with you. But then I also think, we've got a lot of latitude. And what Hyland doesn't know…"

I sat back. "Good point." I hadn't really thought about it that way.

I took a sip of the soup. The warm, salty broth tasted heavenly. What was it about a long day of fresh air that made you so tired and nearly anything tasted good?

"This case though. It's… I don't know… It's like it can't be solved anyway, so why are we here?"

"What do you mean?"

"In the past, we've gone after criminals. We knew who the bad guys were. They knew they were bad guys. Our job was to catch them. But here, these attitudes, the politics. It's like it's ingrained in the culture. There's no bad guy to lock up and throw away the key. No way we're going to make a difference."

"What about Jack Wade?"

I shook my head. "I don't know. If he's up to something, he's covered it well. But I don't think he is. I admit, though, the control action makes me wonder. Do you think ranchers would pay him on the side to completely eradicate the wolves?"

"We should have Greg look into it tomorrow. See if he can

find any sort of financial trail."

"I suppose. I guess, I just don't see it. That feels much more like a fringe conspiracy theory. I don't see a bunch of ranchers getting together late one night in an old barn conjuring up ways to make a few bucks and secretly do away with the wolves. For one thing, they already do it overtly. They feel it's their right to do it."

"I think you're right. The wolves are caught in the middle of a much bigger, much more complicated dispute. There are some deep-seated identity issues involved. It's like ranchers feel as though bringing back wolves was a direct attack on who they are as people. It's more than that though. I was reading about this concept of complexly linked social and ecological systems and how that complexity means that conflicts can become intractable, solutions nearly impossible to achieve, and enforcing even what seems like small actions can have unintended consequences."

"Exactly. You get it. During that whole conversation with Mr. Johnson this morning, I knew there was no way to persuade him. And I could see his point of view. I mean, I do try. I understand exactly what you're saying. Everything he said, every point he made, it made perfect sense. To him. His livelihood is threatened. The wolves are the problem. But there's always that one issue, the one that I can't accept, and that's the utter disregard for life. For the animal's life. His answer, without hesitation, without remorse, is kill it. It's a problem, kill it. When I suggested non-lethal ways to handle wolves, I could see it in his eyes. He saw me as a pie-eyed dreamer. A child. Someone to be pacified because of my ignorance."

Tom sighed. "I could explain the history and formation of modern human nature, but I don't think it would make you feel any better."

"No, it wouldn't. I know I can't change it. And it frustrates the hell out of me. But what I do know is there's a pack of wolves here, right now, about to be slaughtered. What do I do about that?"

He gave me an encouraging nod. "We do what we can. Like you said, we go on ahead with the plan, find this sheepherder, and see what he says. Maybe he'll give us what we need to stop the control action."

I nodded. "Yes. We'll convince him. I mean, you'll convince him. You do the talking."

"If you say so."

"I do."

He rose to put out the fire. "I suppose we should get some sleep." He groaned, rubbing his thigh. "I feel like I'll never walk straight again."

I laughed. I could totally relate. We doused the fire and crawled into our sleeping bags. As I closed my eyes, I smiled. I was glad to have Tom on my team. He was like the wise, supportive uncle I never knew I needed.

Daylight warmed the tent and woke me from my dream. I sat up, rubbed the salty crust from my eyes, and crawled over my sleeping bag and out the zippered door.

The horses were still tied where I'd left them, looking bored.

I fired up the stove and set some water to boil for coffee before I scampered off into the woods to pee.

When I got back, Tom was awake and rolling up the tent.

Within minutes, we were on our way, our thermal mugs filled with cowboy coffee.

The crisp morning air felt refreshing. Somehow, it brought a feeling of optimism. Or maybe it was knowing Tom was on my side. Mike certainly wasn't. And Dalton was AWOL. But having Tom here with me helped a lot. Maybe I wasn't much of a loner after all.

Duchess seemed to enjoy the morning, too. She had a pep in her step, walking along, clip-clop, clip-clop. Maybe she was enjoying the change of scenery. And the quiet. "That's right girl. Let's find that sheepherder, wherever he is," I said, urging her up an incline.

By mid-morning, we came over a rise, and along the sloping side of a basin was a flock of sheep, nearly two-thousand strong. Two big white dogs—Great Pyrenees guard dogs—ran toward us in greeting. They didn't seem bothered by our presence; I assumed because we were on horseback.

The sheep noticed our arrival and moved away from us, the entire flock moving as one in a synchronized motion, like a flock of birds in flight.

Near the top of the basin, a man stood watching us, his face hidden in the shadow of a floppy cotton hat. I waved. He didn't wave back.

"At least we found him," I said to Tom.

I guided Duchess in his direction. As I neared, I couldn't read the expression on his face. I thought he might be glad to see another human. Some of these men spent the entire season out here alone, with no contact other than the occasional provisions delivery from the rancher. Others worked with a partner, but most were alone for months—isolated nomads. Their jobs were twenty-four seven. Keep the sheep moving to new grazing grounds, keep them healthy, and keep them alive.

He was neither alarmed, nor scared. I decided he was the type to take things as they came. He was a small, thin man and looked to be in his sixties. Mr. Johnson had said he'd worked for him for seventeen years.

"Hello," I said and waved again as I approached.

This time he acknowledged me, but still didn't wave back.

I passed his camp—a small tent, a foldable camp stove, canvas bags stuffed with supplies—all of which would regularly get packed up and moved to the next location on the back of his horse and the mule who grazed nearby.

The guard dogs had moseyed away, apparently having come

to the conclusion that we were no threat to the sheep, but two herding dogs, black and white border collies, circled as I dismounted.

"What a beautiful day," I said, trying to engage the man.

He stared.

Maybe he didn't speak English. "Hola."

He gave me the same nod. *Hm.*

I walked toward him. "Mr. Johnson sent us."

That got his attention. He walked to meet me. "Is everything okay?" he asked, his accent heavy.

"Oh yes. We just wanted to talk to you."

Tom came up behind me. "Hello, Hector. Nice to meet you. I'm Tom." He held out a hand. The man took it but seemed unsure. "This is Poppy."

I smiled.

I glanced over at the impression he'd left in the grass. He'd been napping in the morning sun. "We're sorry to interrupt your day."

"How can I help you?"

Tom answered. "Like Poppy said, Mr. Johnson sent us out to talk to you. We just have some questions, about how it's going out here."

"It's fine. Just fine." He crossed his arms in front of his chest. Was our presence putting him on the defensive?

"Mr. Johnson told us you're doing a great job," I said, hoping that would ease his mind.

His expression didn't change.

We needed to get right to the point. "Have you had any trouble lately with wolves?"

"Si," he grinned, showing a missing front tooth. "Las terroristas." *The terrorists.*

Tom glanced at me. He didn't speak Spanish.

"You don't like wolves," I said. A statement.

He let his arms drop to his side. "What's to like? When they kill my sheep, it is very sad."

"There are ways," Tom said, "to keep them from getting your sheep."

"Yes, I have dogs." He pointed at one of the guard dogs, then grinned again. "And a gun."

"But you're alone. You can't watch all night."

The corner of his eyes crinkled with concern. "I am a good herder."

"Oh, no doubt," Tom said in a reassuring voice. "We just thought we'd share some ideas to help make it easier for you."

His eyes flitted from Tom to me then back to Tom. "Like what?"

"South of here, some sheepherders have been using fladry with success. It's a string fence to set up around the sheep once they bed down at night. It has bits of fabric, like little flags, hanging from it that wolves don't like to cross."

Hector crossed his arms again. "You mean, I would have to set it up every night around my sheep?"

"Well, yes." His expression didn't change, so Tom went on. "There are several other options. Some use radio-activated alarms. Some like noisy firecrackers." He glanced at me.

The horses hated them. I couldn't imagine wolves wouldn't act the same.

"More things for me to carry?" Hector said.

Tom looked over at Hector's horse and mule. "Maybe you could get another mule."

"Another animal I have to care for, feed, keep track of."

Tom looked discouraged.

I stepped forward. "Yes, some of the options might take a little bit of extra work, but—"

"Do you know my job?"

I hesitated. "No."

"Do you know that the government requires that Mr. Johnson post for American workers every year before he hires me back again? Do you know what happens? No one in America wants this job. And I am thankful."

"I understand. It's hard work." I looked over at his meager camp. "And lonely, I'm sure."

"I see my family one month of the year."

Tom stepped in. "We don't want to make your job harder, sir. Some of these techniques, while they may seem, at first, to cause more work, they'll pay off in the way they'll keep the wolves at bay."

"At bay?" He lifted his shotgun. "I take care of las terroristas one time. I don't worry about them again."

Suddenly I realized how pointless our trip up the mountain had been. Hector was the last person who'd agree. If Mr. Johnson told him he had to do these things, he would. But why would he volunteer? He had absolutely no incentive. He saw wolves as one thing, a threat to his livestock and therefore a threat to his livelihood.

Mr. Johnson knew it too. He'd sent us on a wild goose chase.

"Thank you for your time, Hector. We're sorry to interrupt your day."

He nodded, seemingly unsure if that would be the end of it.

"Would you point us in the direction of the fastest way to get back to the river where we can cross?"

He explained the path.

"Gracias," I said.

Tom followed. When we were out of earshot, he said, "You surprise me. You gave up so easily."

"He was never going to agree. Why would he?" I frowned. "And Mr. Johnson knew it."

By the time Tom and I got back to Julie's farm, we'd both vowed to never get on the back of a horse again.

"I think my ass has been permanently reshaped," Tom said with a groan.

Julie came out from the house to help us. "How was your

ride? Did you find him?'"

"We did. Thank you so much," I said, sliding off the horse.

Julie took the reins to lead Duchess into the barn. I wasn't sure my legs would hold me upright. I hobbled after her.

"You two look exhausted," she said. "I'll take care of the horses. Don't you worry about it."

"That's very kind," I said.

"Well," she said with a grin, "you paid well for it."

Tom motioned for me to follow him out of the barn. "Let's regroup in the morning," he said.

I wanted nothing more than a hot shower and cool sheets, but the clock was ticking. I shook my head. "Time's running out."

"What can we do yet today?" he asked.

Maybe our trip had been a wild goose chase, but that didn't mean Raina hadn't gleaned something from the interaction with Emmett and Denny. "You go ahead," I said. "I got something to follow up on."

We walked to our cars, which were parked beside the barn, where they'd be out of Julie's way. As we came around the corner, I saw it first—a dead chicken on my hood, the words, "Go home" scrawled in blood on the windshield.

I sighed.

"You've been making friends, I see," Tom said.

My phone beeped. A text message came in from Mike: I've met all the young men here at the ranch. Most are wholesome, polite, law abiding citizens. Bobby and Bart are the exception. They're just a couple of punks. Nobody here likes them either. I've heard no talk of anything illegal or otherwise related. It's time for me to leave this post and move on.

I stared at the dead chicken, trying to tamp down my anger, and typed back: Negative. You stay put.

CHAPTER 14

Raina's van was parked in the same pullout on the back corner of Julie's property. I pulled in far enough that my car was also hidden from view from the road and got out.

A curtain in a side window was pulled back, then quickly fell back into place, and the door was flung open.

"Poppy. How'd it go?"

"How do you think it went?"

"Yeah, I kinda figured."

"You have any more of that tea?"

"Sure," she said. "C'mon in." She held the door open for me.

I went straight for the little couch and flopped on my side. "I'm not cut out for horseback riding."

Raina stifled a grin, then set the tea kettle to boil.

"Tell me you got something out of it," I said.

She shrugged. "Wish I could. I can say that, from my experience so far, he would have gotten riled with that conversation at the diner, like we said, poke the bear. I was as surprised as you were that he was so calm. I guess he knew all along where it was leading."

I sat up. "I'm such a fool."

"Nah, I put you up to it."

"So, I was a fool to follow you?"

She smiled. "I did learn one thing."

"Yeah?" I sat up straight. "Tell me."

"Casey was not happy about it."

"His son Casey? The hunting guide."

"Yeah. Those two do *not* have a good relationship. We were at the Roadhouse. Casey was there, kept looking around. I assume for you. Emmett walked right over to him, told him not to bother, that you'd gone up into the hills with some other guy to talk to Hector. Casey said, 'And you sent her, didn't you?' Emmett shrugged and Casey lost it. I'm not sure what that was about."

"Casey was looking for me?"

She grinned. "Pretty sure. Why? You like him? He is a handsome devil. Emphasis on devil."

"He asked me to go to dinner. I figured I might be able to get some information from him. But why do you call him a devil?"

She thought about it a moment. "I don't know, actually. I guess I figured he's Emmett's kid and you met Denny, his other son. Maybe I shouldn't be so quick to judge."

The teakettle whistled. She poured me a mug and handed it to me, the tea bag floating at the top. "Careful, let that steep a minute."

Exhaustion overcame me. I laid my head back. "Oh Raina, how do you do it? Maybe I don't have the patience to be a journalist, I don't know. This is so frustrating."

She sat down on the couch next to me. "I think your problem is that you have conflicting goals."

I forced myself into an upright position, swished the teabag around in my cup. "What do you mean?"

"Well, a story is a story. You learn what you can about all the aspects of it. Dig deeper if you have to, find people's motivations. But you seem to want them to be what they aren't. You don't want to accept that some people don't care about the wolves at all."

I chewed on my lip. *And they're systematically killing them.*

"It's all part of the bigger story, here. To be a good journalist, you can't get personally invested."

"Someone killed a chicken, left it on my hood, and wrote 'Go home' on my windshield with its blood."

Her lip curled up at the side. "Are you serious?"

"While I was gone to talk to Hector. My car was parked next to Julie's barn."

"Was it one of Julie's chickens?"

I shrugged. "I assume."

"Well, hell."

"Yeah. But actually, I can handle that. It was Bobby or Bart or Carl or Don. Angry cowpokes with pent up frustration. Whatever. What I can't wrap my mind around is that, at any moment, the state government will give the go ahead to kill a whole pack of wolves. And I'm not convinced it's justified."

"So, write about that."

"Sure, okay, but it won't save the wolves."

"It might save some in the future."

"God, you sound just like—" I drew in a breath, let it out. "Never mind."

"Not all journalism is unbiased news. You could write for a conservation organization, if that's where your passion is."

"I'll think about that, thanks." This conversation wasn't going where I needed it to. "Meanwhile, what do we do next?"

"Maybe you should take Casey up on that dinner invitation, and while you're at it, get some info for me. Would you mind? I'm curious about the arrangement with his father. His hunting lodge is on the back corner of Emmett's property. It's his livelihood and they don't get along. That's got to cause some stress."

"I'll see what I can find out," I said, finally taking a sip of the tea.

"Thanks. As for your concern about the state approving the killing of these wolves, well, I wonder if the local wolf supporters know about that," she looked up at me over her mug, eyes full of mock innocence.

A smile formed on my face. "You mean those who would put up a fight."

She grinned. "A call from a journalist for a statement, well, if they didn't already know it was happening—"

"You're a genius."

She moved to the tiny table and opened a laptop. "I'll look them up, you call."

For the next two hours, I called every conservation organization in the state that might be opposed to the control action that would allow Jack Wade to kill that pack of wolves. I might have even mentioned that a rally was forming at the foot of the Capitol steps at noon the next day.

It was nine o'clock before I left Raina's motorhome. I was beat. A hot shower and fluffy bed were calling me.

When I pulled into the drive at Gladys's rooming house, there was another car in the driveway. She must have had another guest.

I parked my car and went in.

Gladys was sitting in her rocker, and on the couch across from her, was Dalton.

CHAPTER 15

He rose as I entered the room.

"Dalton." It was the only word I could get out of my mouth. He hadn't called. Hadn't texted. Nothing. But here he was. *My* Dalton. With those eyes, and those arms, and that smile. His face was bronze from the African sun. A little stubble on his chin. I flushed pink.

I glanced at Gladys. She was enjoying my surprise. She waited a moment too long before pushing herself up from her chair. "I'll leave you two to talk."

"That's all right," I said, finding my voice. I held up a hand to stop her. "He can come up to my room."

She looked at me over her glasses. "This is a boarding house. I ain't running no hourly *mo*-tel."

"Yes, ma'am. I assure you. We're just going to talk. Privately."

She pursed her lips, unsure.

"This way," I said and headed for the stairs. Dalton followed.

As soon as the door shut behind us, I was in his arms. His kiss gave me a burst of adrenaline. "What are you doing here? Why didn't you call? What'd you tell Gladys? Where've you been?"

He stared at me for half a second, then pulled me to him, drugging me with his passion. "Did you miss me?" he whispered in my ear.

"Are you kidding? I wasn't sure if you were coming back."

His lips met mine and I forgot all my questions. Nothing mattered. He was here. With me. Right now.

Finally, he pulled away and gestured toward the door. "I wouldn't doubt if she's outside the door right now, leaning against it with a Dixie cup to her ear."

"You're terrible."

"I got the idea not much happens around here."

I sat down on the bed and pulled him down on top of me as I leaned back. "What'd you tell her?"

"The truth. That I'm madly in love with you and—"

"You are?"

"Yep." He smiled at me. "And we had a fight. And I left. And I had to come out here and find you, so we could kiss and make up."

"How'd you know that wouldn't ruin my cover?"

He kissed me. "I didn't care."

"But what made you think she'd buy it?"

He kissed me again. "I saw the Harlequin romance novel on the end table."

"Ah." I kissed him back. "So, it was a story?"

"Nope."

I paused, looking into his eyes. "It's true?"

"That I love you?"

"Yeah."

"More than anything in this world."

"Me too."

"Me too, what?"

"I love you more than anything in this world."

We couldn't get undressed fast enough. "Shhhh, she'll hear us."

"I can be quiet as a mouse," he said and flipped the light out. "Can you?"

I awoke with a start. The red illuminated numbers on the alarm clock read 5:05.

I nudged Dalton. "Wake up."

He groaned. "What? What's wrong?"

"Nothing. We need to talk."

He opened one eye. "Now?"

"Yeah, now." I flipped on the light.

He pulled the pillow over his head. "I was kinda hoping to have a day or two to get over my jet lag."

"Yeah, Africa is a long way to go."

His eyes shot open. "How'd you—Chris."

"Yeah, Chris. He's my best friend and we were both worried."

"Worried?"

"Okay, he was worried. I was mad."

"Uh-huh."

"Why'd you go to Africa?"

He glanced at the clock. "Do we need to talk about this right now?"

"Yes."

"Fine." He sat up. "I need to use the head first."

"I guess that's fair."

He got out of bed, looked around. "Where is it?"

I got up, handed him my fuzzy pink robe, and opened the door. "Down the hall."

He plodded across the wood floor. I got back into bed. When he came back, he snuggled up to me like a spoon.

"How'd you know where to find me anyway?" I asked.

"Greg."

"What else did Greg tell you?"

"He said you were posing as a journalist and brought me up to speed on some of the players." He rolled me over. "He said Hyland put you on point for this op. Congratulations."

"Thanks. Though I'm totally blowing it. I don't even know whether there's been any criminal activity, except for poisoning wolves with strychnine, which she told me not to bother investigating. Can you believe that?"

He frowned.

"So, what do you need me to do?"

"Oh no. You're trying to change the subject. You're going to tell me about Africa."

He shoved the pillow against the headboard and sat up, leaning against it. "Fine. I thought you might be getting an idea in your head to go. It was the way you were asking Jesse in Bimini. So, I decided that, since I was due a vacation, and felt like maybe you and I needed a little space, I went to see what I could find out. That's all."

"And? What'd you find out?"

He looked me in the eyes. "Poppy, I don't think—"

I shoved myself up to a seated position. "Oh for godssake, just tell me."

"You're dad was killed by poachers. I know that."

"Do you know who?"

"Not the individual, but I know what group and—"

"Did you talk to the authorities? How'd you find out? You weren't there long. There must have been—"

"Poppy, take a breath."

I drew in a sharp breath. "Don't tell me to take a breath. This is my dad we're talking about."

He stared at me, contemplating something. "It's not so much the who that matters, but the why."

"The why?"

"Poppy." He inhaled, a long deep breath. Then exhaled. "Your dad wasn't an innocent bystander. He was undercover."

I sat back and stared at him. "What?" *Undercover?* "What are you saying?"

"An NGO was trying to get intel on a local gang known for trafficking ivory. Your dad signed on to help."

"He did? He was actually…he wasn't…with his photography?"

"No. He wasn't. Well, he was. He used that as a cover."

"Why would he do that? He didn't have any training for that sort of thing. He didn't have fighting skills or weapons training or…" I shook my head. "I can't believe this." I got up from the bed and paced back and forth. "This can't be right."

"It wouldn't have mattered," Dalton said, a softness to his voice.

I spun around to face him. "What do you mean?"

"It was a fight he couldn't win."

I sat down on the bed, suddenly exhausted. "What do you mean?"

"He wasn't just outgunned, or outnumbered. Ivory is the currency of those gangs. It's ingrained in their culture. One man isn't going to stop that. You know that. We've talked about this over and over again. The only thing that can stop that level of organized crime is going all the way to the top. China, Africa—their leaders need to make the change. Bigger fines, greater punishments, actually enforce the laws they do have. Stop the demand. Make buying it the punishable crime."

My hands started to shake. "So, you're saying he died for nothing."

His face paled. "No. I…"

I turned away. "Still. Some*one* killed him."

"Poppy, I don't—"

My phone beeped. A text message came in from Greg: *The control action is now before the Governor.*

Dammit!

I turned to Dalton. "What'd you say? About the change? With the leaders?"

"I…" He shook his head.

"This whole op, us being here, it's bullshit. It isn't about the wolves. It's about money and who controls what." I punched in Hyland's number. "Screw that. I can play politics too."

She answered on the third ring. "Agent McVie."

"I need a meeting with the governor."

"That is definitely not going to happen."

"The governor is about to sign a control action, allowing Mr. Wade to kill that entire pack of wolves. I've got wind that a protest rally is forming outside the capitol building today. Now, if this thing blows up, it's going to be a mess. I would think the governor would want to at least be made aware of the situation before signing."

"And what is the situation?"

I saw the thermal-imaging video. It was wolves. They'd done it. But something wasn't right. It just wasn't. I knew it in my gut. I had no proof. But I knew it.

I glanced at Dalton. He was shaking his head.

"The situation is, I'm in the middle of an investigation. I don't have all the answers yet, but there's a reason you sent us here. Some things don't add up. I have reason to believe there's a land dispute in the middle of it all."

There was silence on the other end of the line. "And how does a land dispute—"

"I don't know yet. That's the point. Just imagine how the press will have a heyday when they find out later that gunning down all those wolves wasn't justified, that the governor had been manipulated. All I'm saying is, we should get a chance to finish the investigation before any lethal action is taken. Isn't that reasonable? I would think the governor would be thankful when we save his neck. Now, this is a Presidential task force. Don't we have any influence here?"

"I'll call you back," she said and the line went dead.

I flopped on my back, staring at the ceiling. "Seriously?"

"That was risky," Dalton said.

"Well, I can't sit back and—"

"You continue to amaze me." He was looking at me with those eyes. "That brain of yours. And that heart." The edge of his lips curved up into a grin. "C'mon." He tugged me toward him and wrapped his arms around me. "You've done what you could."

"It's not going to be enough."

"We'll see."

He flipped off the light and wrapped his arms around me.

I lay there for a moment, enjoying his embrace, but thoughts of my dad kept me on edge.

What had he gotten himself tangled up in? Why would he take that kind of risk? And why…?

I had so many questions. My father wasn't a trained agent. He wasn't even a fighter. He was a wildlife photographer. Why would he think he could go up against a crime syndicate like those trafficking in ivory?

Why Dad? Why would you do that?

And leave me all alone.

CHAPTER 16

The phone woke me. I sat up. It was Hyland.

I answered, "Agent McVie."

"You've got an appointment tomorrow at two. The action will be held until then."

"Thank you," I said, surprised.

She disconnected.

Dalton sat up beside me. "Now what?"

"Now what is right? What do I do with you?"

"I can hang out here, be your boy toy."

"I like that idea." I placed a peck on his lips. "But I'm not sure Gladys will. Maybe you should find somewhere else to stay."

"Oh, I bet Gladys would be sorry to see us go. She hasn't had this much excitement since Nixon resigned."

"Yeah, but, actually, I need to follow up on a dinner date." I clenched my teeth together, waiting. Would he be upset? "A boyfriend will kinda cramp my style."

He laughed, an honest, hearty chuckle. "I get it. I can see when I'm getting shot down. You're breaking my heart, babe. Who's the lucky guy?"

"His name is Casey. He owns a hunting guide service and lodge. He's actually your primary person of interest. I was hoping you could play the big, rich elk hunter, see what you can find out."

"I can do that."

"Hold on. It's late enough. I'll give him a call." I found his number on his web site and dialed. Clicking the phone to speaker, I held my finger in front of my lips, signaling Dalton to keep quiet.

Casey answered on the third ring.

"Hey, this is Poppy. From the Roadhouse."

"Well, hello. I'm so glad to hear from you."

"I felt bad about the other night. I didn't mean to be rude, is all. I wanted you to know that, if the offer still stands, I'd love to have dinner with you."

"I'm glad. How about tonight?"

I winked at Dalton. "Um, sure. Where should I meet you?"

"Aren't you staying at Gladys's place?"

"Yes."

"I'll pick you up at six."

"Where will we be going?" I hadn't seen a restaurant for miles, save for the diner and the Roadhouse.

"It's a surprise."

Dalton shook his head.

"Ooooh. I like that," I said, enjoying Dalton's frown. "I'll see you then. But so you know, I'm a vegetarian."

"You're what?"

"A vegetarian. I don't eat meat."

"I know what a vegetarian is. What I don't understand, is why."

"Well, then we'll have something to talk about. Bye." I disconnected.

"I don't like it," Dalton said.

"Don't like what?"

"A surprise. Where's he taking you? In his car. I don't like it. It's not safe."

"You're being paranoid." I eyed him. "And jealous?"

"I'll have Greg tracking your every move on satellite."

I held up the phone. "He already does."

"Right. Well, I'm going to know where you are every second."

"Okay, now you're sounding creepy."

"Yes, I'm the creepy jealous boyfriend. That could work."

I stared. "I'm on point. I get to decide your role."

"Oh right. What's my role?"

"Okay, the creepy jealous boyfriend. But give me some time to get some information out of him first."

"You better hurry. I want my girlfriend back."

At noon, I checked the Boise TV stations. A few hundred protestors had gathered at the capitol building, carrying picket signs and walking in circles.

Dalton had sent an email through Casey's web site, inquiring about hunting parties, then sneaked out without Gladys seeing him. He drove south to get a room at the same roadside motel where Tom was staying.

Tom was diligently canvassing the community, door to door, talking with ranchers about non-lethal methods for predator control and gauging their attitudes. Maybe someone would stand out.

Mike was stuck on the back of a horse for another day. I hoped. Was I being kinda bitchy about him? *Who cares*. He was where I needed him to be.

I stopped by the diner for an ice tea, but nothing was going on there, so I headed back to my room and took my time with yoga and a long bath before I got ready for my dinner date. Getting Casey to talk was my best option at this point. If anyone knew who was doing what around here, it was him. But would he tell me? How would I get him to talk?

Promptly, at six on the dot, Casey pulled into the drive. He came up to the door and knocked. I was waiting in the living room. When he came inside, Gladys gave me that look, the one that said, in her day, you didn't go out with one boy the next day after another had come to visit. I fully expected Dalton's visit to get back to Casey right away. If I needed charm on my side, I had one shot at this before things went south.

"Wow, you are a sight for sore eyes," he said.

Was that a compliment? "Thank you," I said with a coy smile.

He tipped his hat at Gladys. "Ma'am."

"You're just as handsome as ever," she said, a dreamy look in her eyes.

"Thank you, ma'am."

"You kids be good, now," she said as we scooted out the door.

Casey drove a cobalt blue Ford F-150. It shined tonight from a fresh wash. He walked me around to the passenger side, opened the door for me, and closed it once I was seated inside. *Hm. A gentleman. Unlike his creep brother.*

He slipped into the driver's seat and fired up the engine. It whirred to life.

"I think Gladys might have a crush on you," I said, grinning at him.

"Gladys has had it hard since her old man died ten years ago." He moved the gear shift into reverse. "She takes in any overflow, you know, extra hunters we have when the lodge is full, but I doubt she gets many other boarders. I don't know how she makes end meet."

"Yes, I've been the only one here all week."

He turned his head to look out the back window as he backed up.

"So, where are we headed?"

As he made the turn onto the road, slowed and shifted into drive, he smiled at me. "I told you, it's a surprise."

He was heading north, toward town. He made a right at the next road, rolling through the stop, then left at the main road. He slowed as we passed through town, but didn't pull in to the diner. North of town, there wasn't much on the map. Certainly not another town. All roads going that way eventually spread out into the hills and spider-webbed into two-tracks that went into Nez Perce National Forest land.

Another mile or so up the road, he slowed for a cow, standing in the middle of the road. He punched a number into his phone. "Sally, tell Jed he's got one loose. Standing right in the middle of the road." A pause. "No, I can wait." Another pause. "All right then." He put the truck in park, got out, leaving the door open, and ran at the animal, waving his hat in front of him, causing it to rear back and trot off the road into the ditch.

When he got back into the truck, I said, "That was a kind thing to do."

He looked at me, shrugged. "Yeah, well. That's what neighbors do." He shifted the truck into gear, pressed on the gas pedal, and we continued on.

He seemed pensive, reticent. Strange. He'd seemed eager to chat when we'd met at the Roadhouse.

Another eight miles up the road, with not one word from Casey, we passed New Hope Farm, on the right. "Do you know Julie?" I asked.

He nodded.

"Wolves got her chickens."

"I heard. That's too bad. She seems like a nice lady."

"What do you think about what she's doing there, how she's building a farm for at-risk kids?"

He turned to look at me. "What are you talking about?"

"New Hope Farm. She's trying to build a sustainable farm where at-risk kids from the city can come for the summer to learn life skills and stuff."

His expression turned to surprise. "I didn't know that."

That was odd. "Wow, I thought the grapevine was strong around here."

He seemed bothered by the fact that he didn't know it, yet tried to hide that from me. "I knew she had inherited the farm, but I didn't know her plans."

"Yeah, well. Who knows what will happen now, what with her chickens being killed by those wolves."

He simply nodded, gave no comment.

Past the Johnson ranch, he turned right onto a gravel road.

"There's a restaurant out here?" I asked. I knew where he was taking me. Greg had said his hunting lodge was on the back corner of the Johnson property.

"Better."

He turned down a two-track that led into the woods. It wound back and forth, up and down, the truck bouncing over roots and bumps, until we came upon the lodge.

The lodge wasn't at all what I expected. I'd been to a hunting lodge in Alaska, where Dalton and I had gone to investigate a bear poacher. That lodge stood out from the landscape, all pretentious in its supposed grandeur, an oasis where the hunters didn't actually have to *rough it*. This lodge had been built by someone who loved the land. It seemed to blend into the hillside, the timbers an outgrowth of the living forest.

Casey parked next to another truck, got out, and hurried around to my side to open the door for me.

As I stepped out, I caught the scent of burning wood and baking bread on the cool air.

Casey took my hand and led me through the front entrance, which framed a hand-hewn, solid wood door.

"That's beautiful," I said. "The craftsmanship is amazing."

"Thank you," he said.

I didn't hide my surprise. "Did you build it?"

"Yep, from the ground up."

"The entire lodge?"

He grinned. "Yep. Me and my uncle."

A fire crackled in the fireplace, the focal point of the main room. Above, hung on the stone chimney, was the head of a six-by-six elk. Leather couches adorned with red flannel pillows were arranged on either side of a hand-made coffee table.

Other than the glass-eyed elk staring down at us, the room

felt quite cozy.

"I've got eight rooms, besides mine."

"So, you guide eight hunters at a time?"

"Sometimes more. Like I said, if we do, they usually stay with Gladys. But we don't hunt right here anyway. I bring up horses from the ranch, down in the valley. During the season, we'll head out for a week at a time, into the mountains. I have a cook, a couple other guides, a few horse wranglers. We set up a base camp with a kitchen and tents for everyone."

At an average of $5000 a hunt, Casey was making good money at this, even having to pay those other workers, though he had a limited season.

A man came around the corner from another room, an apron tied at his waist. Tall and thin, he looked European. The way his eyes took me in, definitely French.

"Poppy, you'll be glad to meet René. He's our camp cook and, lucky for you, he was available tonight."

René shook my hand.

"If it was left to me," Casey went on, "we'd be eating Dinty Moore stew out of the can."

René nodded and gave me a wink. "It's true." To Casey he said, "Everything's ready, like we talked about." He untied the apron from his waist. "I'm going to head out."

"Thanks, René."

"Nice to meet you," I said to his retreating form. He wasn't being rude. He was leaving us alone.

Casey led me into the dining room, where candles burned on the table. Two place settings had already been set out on the rustic table.

"Wow, this is really nice," I said.

"Go ahead and have a seat." Casey moved toward the kitchen. In a moment, he was back with a basket of warm bread.

A bottle of wine was on the table, a corkscrew next to it. Beaujolais-Villages. Nice choice. Was that René's doing as well? "Shall I open the wine?" I asked.

"Sure, go ahead," he said over his shoulder.

I popped the cork and poured two glasses.

Casey appeared from the kitchen again and set a hot dish in front of me and one in front of him. The dish was filled with bright, chunky vegetables and the fragrance of garlic and herbs. He tossed the oven mitt back into the kitchen before taking his seat. He looked me in the eyes, "Okay, I admit. I have no idea what this is. I told René something vegetarian." He looked down at his meal, examining it. "I was going to pretend that I'd cooked it, from scratch, all by myself, to impress you, but then I realized, one question and my whole façade would crumble."

I smiled. This man really was adorable. "It's ratatouille," I said.

I could tell by his expression, he had no idea what that was.

"It's a French summer stew of vegetables. You'll love it."

"If you say so." He dug in with his fork.

After I'd savored a few delectable bites, I swirled the wine around in my glass and said, "So, do you mind if I ask you some questions?"

"Are you nervous?" His eyes twinkled. He liked the idea that I was nervous.

"Uh. No. I feel very comfortable with you. Why do you ask?"

"The way you're fiddling with your glass."

I looked down at my wine. "Oh, no. I'm aerating it."

"You're what?"

"Well, you might as well know. I'm kind of a wine snob. I love wine. And see, it tastes better if you give it some air. Like this." I gave it a twirl again.

"Really? I didn't know that. I guess I'm just a country boy."

"Maybe. I bet you know a lot of things I don't know." *Like who's killing the wolves.* "It's just something I like and had the opportunity to learn about. I worked as a sommelier when I was in college."

His head tilted to the side.

"That's a wine steward. I worked in a really upscale restaurant and chose the wines we purchased, matching them with the menu offerings."

"Oh." He looked down at his food, poked it with his fork, then took another bite.

"So, do you mind if I ask you some questions?

He shook his head. "I figured you would. You seem like the kind of woman who doesn't give up easily. You've got a story to write, right?"

"Right." I hesitated. "What made you want to be a hunting guide?"

"Actually, I wanted to be a pilot. But it's hard to run a ranch when you're halfway across the world, as my father put it."

"Is that what you plan to do? Run a ranch?"

"Hell no. My brother Denny will. It's his thing."

"I don't understand. Why couldn't you be a pilot then?"

"You don't know my father."

I gave him a sympathetic smile. "Fair enough. So, you chose hunting guide."

"A more accurate statement would be, I chose against ranching."

I nodded. I could see how Emmett Johnson was a man you didn't want to cross.

"I do like hunting, though," he said.

"At the stock show, when I asked you about wolf hunting, you said, the government *letting* you hunt them isn't going to have any effect. What did you mean by that?"

"Elk hunting isn't what it used to be. Culling a few wolves here and there isn't going to bring it back. There's a much bigger problem."

"What was it like before?"

"Before the wolves? When I was a kid, wrangling horses for my uncle, he could set up a camp, take a guy out in the morning, and guarantee a trophy bull by ten. A little bugling, and in they'd come. Now, I'm lucky to find one for every five hunters I take out. I suppose I should be grateful I'm still in business. Eight other outfitters have folded in this county alone since I was a kid.

"That's not the only problem, though," he went on. "Fewer elk also means fewer licenses issued. I got customers who want to come, but can't get the license. It limits my ability to make a living. I rely on non-resident licenses, the guys who'll pay big to come out here, be taken to the right spot, so they can pull the trigger and take home a trophy. They're expectations are still like the old days.

"Between the guides, my cook, the wranglers, my horses, the lodge, then all the government red tape, I got some serious overhead. Since we hunt on national forest land, I pay an annual fee as well as a big game outfitter's license. Then there's the insurance. Not just any insurance. *Special* insurance. And they change the regulations all the time, I swear, just to encourage me to give it up." He frowned, stared down at his food. "I'm sorry. I don't mean to unload on you."

"It's all right," I said. "Really. Go ahead. I'm curious about all this."

"You asked about wolves. Well, it goes without saying, I'm losing my livelihood to the wolves, partially, but more specifically the government's bad policies around the whole issue."

He set to work on his ratatouille, as if suddenly he felt he'd said enough.

He didn't realize, but he'd become another suspect in the long line of those who wanted the wolves gone. I didn't believe he was poisoning the wolves. It didn't fit his personality, nor would it solve his problem. But he probably knew who was. He probably knew a lot more than that. Especially what was going on between his father and Julie.

"I met your father," I said.

He raised his gaze to look right at me.

"We had quite the conversation about wolves."

"I heard he sent you to talk to Hector."

"Yeah, turned out to be a wild goose chase."

He rolled his eyes. "That's my pop. Crafty old bastard. If you'd have asked me, I would have told you not to trust him."

"He shares your loathing of wolves."

"I don't hate wolves. I just…"

I waited.

He frowned. "It's complicated."

"That's for sure." *Maybe I should just ask him flat out. But would he tell me?* It was a long shot. But I needed a Hail Mary right now. Even if the Governor stopped the control action, someone would still kill them. They'd find other ways.

"Someone's been poisoning the wolves, the ones right out here, practically in your backyard. Strychnine," I said.

He blew a puff of breath out of the side of his mouth. "Jesus."

"Do you know who it is?"

He stared at me. Said nothing.

"Would you tell me if you did?"

He sat back in his chair. "Well, it's not me."

"It wasn't an accusation."

"You don't understand the way of life around here."

"You're right. I don't get it at all. Please help me understand. Why does everyone hate wolves so much?"

"Are you for real? I just told you. I'm losing my livelihood to the wolves. You saw for yourself, what they did to Julie's chickens. Destroyed her livelihood. Even the ranchers, my father, as much as I hate to be in alignment with his way of thinking, they threaten his livestock, every day. It's a constant battle."

"But I don't think—"

"They're just animals. Like any other. If you got a dog that bites, be rid of it."

And there it was. Animals. No right to live if they didn't serve humans. Cause a problem, and you're gone. *Man* shall have *dominion*.

I drew in a deep breath and slowly exhaled. "I see your point. Thanks for clarifying that for me."

I took a sip of my wine, poked at my meal with my fork.

Casey said nothing.

I couldn't let it go. "But still, poisoning them, indiscriminately like that, is inhumane."

"I don't know anything about it. If I did, well,—" he sighed "—I probably wouldn't tell you."

"Fair enough. Thanks for being honest."

He half-smiled, resigned. He rose from his chair. "René made some dessert, too."

As he disappeared into the kitchen, I clenched my hands into fists. *Dammit.* I was getting nowhere. At least maybe I could get the scoop on the land dispute for Raina. Unless Casey clammed up completely. At this point, I was pretty sure he didn't think a second date was going to happen.

He came back out, carrying two ramekins of crème brûlée.

"Oh my," I said when he set mine in front of me.

"Yeah, I think René was having fun in my kitchen."

I spooned some into my mouth. "Ooooh, that is goooood."

"I'm glad you like it."

"So, I didn't mean to be Debbie Downer. New subject? You mentioned hunting with your uncle. Where's he now?"

"My great-uncle, actually. He passed away years ago. Died of a broken heart."

"Really?" I sat back, surprised. "I can honestly say I've never heard a man say that before."

"It's true. He loved the ranch as much as I do, which is to say, he hated it. He could've left though." He shook his head.

"Why didn't he?"

"He was in love. All those years. With another man's wife."

"You're kidding. Did she know?"

He nodded. "Everyone did."

"But she didn't love him back?"

"It was more complicated than that."

"How?"

"She was an only child. Her parents died in an accident, and the ranch went to her and her husband. If she divorced, she'd lose everything and she was a dyed-in-the-wool cowgirl."

"So, he died, a lonely old man? What ever happened to her?"

"Oh, she's still around. A widow now. No kids. She still lives on the ranch, though it's not a working ranch anymore. She runs a boarding house there now."

My eyes grew wide with realization. "Gladys?"

"No other."

"Huh." I remembered the way she looked at Casey when he came into the house. "You must look just like your uncle when he was your age."

"I reckon I do."

"So"—*here goes*—"this parcel was your uncle's? You built the house together, then you inherited it when he died?"

He shook his head. "I wish. My father owns it all. I made the mistake of believing him once."

"When you built this lodge?"

"Then too."

"Are you saying—?"

"It's a long story." He stood, picked up the dirty dishes from the table and headed for the kitchen. I rose to follow him. "No, you sit. Relax."

"All right." This didn't feel right. None of this. Casey's relationship with his father wasn't something I was going to figure out tonight. And there was no way I was going to get any details on the land issues.

Someone rapped on the door.

Casey came out of the kitchen, a quizzical look on his face.

"I wonder who that could be? No one comes out here."

He went to the door. I rose and followed him. He drew the door open, and on the porch, stood Dalton, all dressed up like a Texas billionaire.

"Hello there." He flashed his best disarming smile. "Sorry to bother you. I'm Dalton, sent you the email this morning. I just have a short time to visit, and I know how folks don't always check their email regularly, you know, when it's not the season and all, and I thought, what the hell, I'd just stop on by." He looked at me, then back to Casey. "I hope I'm not interrupting anything."

"Actually—" Casey said.

Dalton pushed in. "Wowweee. This is exactly what I'm looking for. I want to bring my men out for a hunt, a sales incentive kinda thing, and this place is perfect." He looked Casey in the eye. "It sure has charm." He slapped him on the shoulder. "A man's kinda lodge. I just have a few questions though, like how far to the nearest private airstrip. My jet can land on a pretty short strip, but if not, I suppose we can always shuttle with the helicopter. Wow, look at that elk. You shoot that yourself? Man, that's exactly what I'm talking about. So how many men can you handle? I got twelve guys. Course, I suppose, if we had to, we could split that up, but I'd prefer not to, you know, for the bonding."

"I'd be happy to discuss it with you. But right now—"

"Oh, I get it. I did interrupt something. Well, my apologies."

"It's all right," I said. "We were just about to call it a night."

Casey reluctantly agreed.

Did I see a hint of a grin? "Well, I can come back in the morning, if that'd be better."

"Yes, why don't you do that?" Casey said.

"I'll head back out then. Do you need a ride, little lady? I don't mind. I gotta head back south. There ain't nothing north of here, as far as I can see."

"No, thank you," Casey said. "I'll take her home."

"It's no trouble. Save you a trip."

Casey shook his head. "Thank you, but, with all respect, I'm not sending my girl off in a car with a perfect stranger."

Dalton looked pained, then his expression changed. "I guess I can respect that. Indeed. I'll see you in the morning then."

Casey shut the door behind him. He turned to me, his brow slumped with exhaustion. "God, I hate guys like that."

CHAPTER 17

The drive to Boise gave me time to think. It would have been nice to have Dalton with me. I needed his advice. This whole operation had been a train wreck from the start. I needed to save these wolves and get out. I'd be lucky if I still had a job. Jack Wade wasn't falsifying anything. I knew it the first moment I met him. I should have packed up the team then and told Hyland to send us on the next one. But I couldn't walk away from the wolves.

These wolves couldn't catch a break and neither could I.

But now I had this one chance. If I couldn't get the Governor to agree, it would all be over.

I had no idea what I was going to say.

Diplomacy. Facts. The art of persuasion. *I can do this.*

When I arrived at the capitol building, I was glad to see some hardy protestors out again today.

I found the office suites of the Governor and was kindly directed to a posh waiting room with leather seats and fresh-cut lilies in a glass vase on the table.

Soon, a man, about forty years old, in a suit that fit like he'd just walked from the tailor's shop, came into the room. "Agent McVie?"

I rose. "Yessir."

He held out a hand. I shook it. "I'm Ted Montgomery. Please follow me."

Down the hall, I could see dead ahead, an ornately carved wooden door. A glass window above read, Office of the Governor.

Ted made a sharp right turn and I followed him into a small office with a desk and two chairs. He gestured for me to be seated in one of the chairs, then sat down behind the desk. A brass name plaque on the desk read, *Ted Montgomery*.

"How can I help you?" he said.

I remained standing. "I have an appointment to speak with the governor."

"I know. How can I help you?"

I stared. "You can take me to speak with the governor."

A grin formed at the corner of his mouth. "Yeah, it doesn't work that way. I'm his assistant. You can give me the information and I'll make sure he gets it."

I crossed my arms. "Yeah, it doesn't work that way," I said, trying not to sound like I was mocking him. "I represent the President. Of the United States. I was told I would speak with the governor and that's who I will speak with about this matter."

He rose, smoothed his pant legs, and muffled a huff. "Ma'am. I don't care who you are. Today, you speak with me."

Damn.

His expression changed. "I assure you. I will hear you out and take it to the governor. That's my job."

I unclenched my teeth and slowly lowered myself into the chair.

"I understand you're here to discuss the matter of a control action, requested by the Wildlife Services agent, a—" he looked down at some paperwork on this desk "—a Mr. Jack Wade."

"Yessir."

"It says here he's requested the permit to include aerial means."

My stomach dropped. *He wants to use a helicopter?*

"And what's the problem?"

"I'm a federal agent assigned to a Presidential task force. We investigate criminal activity that involves animal issues.

In that county, in one concentrated area, wolf depredation has increased ten-fold over the last year. Statistically, that is, well, way out of whack. I was sent here to find out why, particularly, if it's true or not. Since the state government reimburses ranchers for the livestock losses due to wolf kills, we suspected these might be false claims."

"Have you considered it's simply because more people have become aware of the reimbursement program and are encouraged to report?"

I ignored the hint of condescension in his voice. "Then it would follow that claims would increase across the state. This is concentrated in one area."

"Maybe someone over there has a big mouth and is telling everyone to file. Or maybe there are more wolves."

I stared a moment, holding back the words that came to mind.

"Besides, if it's false claims that are your concern, that would be a state matter. Why the task force?"

"We suspected the claims might have originated with Mr. Wade, a federal employee."

"I see. And is that the case?"

I sat back. "I don't know yet."

"Well, Miss McVie—"

"Special Agent McVie." *Jerk.*

He paused. "Well, Special Agent McVie, I went through his reports. There's quite a bit of detail, all of which would be hard to fake. There are photos and other compelling evidence. His reports are quite thorough. It seems like a lot of trouble to go through to, what, get a kickback on the reimbursements? And if so, the ranchers making the claims would also be in violation. That would mean he's got an entire criminal enterprise going on there. Is that what you're suggesting?"

"No. The evidence doesn't suggest that at this point."

"Well, what does it suggest?" He spoke with the patience of one who thinks he's giving someone enough rope to hang themselves.

"It would be premature to speculate."

"I see." He placed his elbows on his desk, interlaced his fingers, and looked straight at me with that smarmy look. "Okay. Why are you here?"

"The politics surrounding these wolves—"

He laughed. That annoying, I've-heard-this-crap-before laugh. "You don't have to tell me about the politics of wolves. Just tell me why you're here."

Okay, asshole. "I'm concerned that if you allow the control action, and we find out that those wolves were all killed under false pretenses, and you could have stopped it, you'll have their blood on your hands."

He laughed again. "Oh, spare me."

Why are all politicians so arrogant? They had the power to make change, to do what's right. With one decision, they could change the fate of these animals. But all his boss cared about was getting re-elected and—*Wait.* I thought a moment. *That's it.* I got up from my chair and moved to the window, looking out at the Capitol steps. "Did you notice the protestors out there today?"

"Do you think I care about a few protestors?"

I turned to face him. "No. I don't think you care at all. They're not *your* constituents. But I bet your boss cares." I took off, out the door, and marched right down to the Governor's office. I pushed through the heavy wooden door. "Excuse me, Mr. Governor."

The man at the desk looked up at me.

Without hesitation, I sailed right toward him. "I'm Special Agent Poppy McVie, here on behalf of the President. I know you're very busy, but what I have to say can't wait."

Mr. Montgomery was right behind me. "John, sorry. She wouldn't—"

The governor held up his hand. His eyes raked over me. "Well, well."

He said it as though I'd been hired for his afternoon quickie.

He rose from the chair, and with the flick of a hand, dismissed his assistant.

Goodbye, Teddy-boy. I stood taller. "Thank you, sir."

His eyes took another run, looking me up and down. The man was at least sixty, his gray hair combed into perfection. He flashed his shiny teeth. "Did Ted not give you a warm welcome?"

"Ted," I said, "doesn't seem to understand the gravity of the situation."

"Ah," he said with a grin and gestured for me to take a seat. I sat.

He perched on the edge of his desk and braced his elbow on his thigh, leaning forward, his full attention on me. "Please explain."

"You have a request on your desk for a control action, basically permission to gun down a pack of wolves from a helicopter."

"Do I?" He feigned ignorance.

"You know you do. My boss called from the President's office requesting this meeting about that very issue."

"Ah, yes. That issue."

"Yes, that issue." He thought he was going to placate me and send me back out the door. "I'm the investigating agent and I'm concerned that those wolves are being killed under false pretenses. It would behoove you to hold off on signing that control action, to give me time to prove it, or, when I do, you'll have their blood on your hands."

"Uh-huh." He leaned back, sitting up straighter. He still didn't look like he cared one bit.

He would. "I don't know if you've looked out your window today, but—"

"It's a gorgeous day, isn't it?"

Was he trying to fluster me? "I'm referring to the protestors on the Capitol steps."

"Yes, it's unfortunate that sometimes we have to make

unpopular decisions. We can't please everyone."

"I agree. Sometimes those decisions really bite you in the ass."

His eyebrows shot up. Now I had his attention.

I was going for broke, taking a stab in the dark. What governor didn't have his sights set on the White House? "I would imagine that killing a whole pack of wolves, from a helicopter…" I tsk, tsked for effect and got up and went to the window. "They're not going to like that. *Especially* if it's unwarranted."

"A few protesters aren't—"

"Oh, I didn't mean them. Didn't you see what's out there? Behind the protestors?" I waved him over but he didn't budge from his perch. "A news van. With a video camera." I spun around. "You know those guys are using drones now? And I bet drone footage of a helicopter, swooping down out of the sky, with a gunman on board, taking out a pack of wolves will make for great television." I paused, letting the image sink in. "That kind of press wouldn't look good. It wouldn't look good at all."

"I don't think you have an understanding of my constituents."

"Oh, I think I do." I crossed my arms in front of my chest. "I've received a genuine cowboy welcome since I arrived, complete with angry threats, inciting my horse to rear, and a dead chicken on the hood of my car."

He didn't blink, didn't say anything.

"Here's the thing. The removal of wolves from the endangered species list here in Idaho, and Montana and Wyoming for that matter, has been accomplished mostly due to the lobbying efforts of the livestock industry, *your* constituents."

He shook his head, now amused. "And?"

"Here's the part you're missing." *You arrogant son of a bitch.* "Sure, here in Idaho, killing wolves gets you votes. Except from those protestors out front, of course. But on a national stage?" I shook my head. "They'll run that footage twenty-four seven. Like I said. It makes for great television. High-powered rifles, a helicopter swooping down, military-style. The wolves won't even have a sporting chance."

His eyes narrowed. "Are you threatening me? That you'll go to the press?"

"I don't have to." I pointed at the window. "They're already here. Someone's been paying attention. And it hasn't been you."

I had him thinking. He stood up. "You have no idea what a political hotbed this is. You want me to *support* wolves? You must be nuts. Pro-wolf activists who speak out against the livestock industry are guaranteed to receive death threats. They're constantly harassed, their tires slashed, homes vandalized. These guys get their windows busted out with bricks in the night." His expression became more intense. "They threaten their *children*. You have no idea what you're asking."

"All I'm saying is give me time to finish my investigation. That seems reasonable, doesn't it? Avoid all that possible political fallout, either way. Simply hold off on signing that control action. Find a way to delay it."

He wrung his hands, then sat back down on the corner of his desk.

"Two days." He raised a finger and wagged it at me. "You've got two days. That's it. At eight a.m. Friday morning, that helicopter is taking flight."

I wasn't to my car yet when my phone rang. It was Hyland.

"How'd it go?"

"The governor was…"

"Was what?"

"He gave me two days. That's it."

"Two days? Well. You just created a ticking time bomb for yourself."

"Yeah, I know. Wait. What do you mean?"

"Now that you brought in the governor, it's on you. You better have a case."

I stopped in my tracks. "What are you saying? That my job is on the line?"

"You're the one who wanted to play politics." The line went dead

Shit!

Great. Just great.

I sent a group text to Dalton, Tom, and Mike, asking them to drop everything and meet me at Dalton's motel room.

Dammit! Dammit! Dammit!

What was I going to do? My suspect wasn't a suspect. I had no other leads. As far as I could tell, there was nothing criminal going on. Except for the poisoning, of course, which no one cared about, because it wasn't even a crime. I'd taken a chance, to save these wolves, and it was going to blow up in my face.

Long after dark, I pulled into the motel parking lot. They were waiting in Dalton's room.

I raised my hand to knock on the door and it swung open. "C'mon in," Tom said.

I hustled in.

"What happened?" Dalton asked.

Mike sat in the only chair with his arms across his chest, glaring at me, expecting to hear how I'd messed up.

"I went to talk to the governor. He agreed to sit on the control action for two days."

"What's that even mean?" Mike asked. "What's the point? As far as I can tell, we don't have a case. You haven't found anything."

"Well, I'm not sure about that," I said, trying to keep my cool. I wanted to smack that smirk off his face.

"Unless you've been holding out on us."

Tom, always the diplomatic one, held up his hands. "Okay,

let's hear her out and then work this through together."

Mike gave him a reluctant nod.

"Poppy, start from the beginning. Tell us everything you know."

I did. I told them about my conversation with Bobby and Bart, about Gladys, about Julie and her chickens, about Sannyu, the dog, being poisoned, about my trip to find the dead wolf with Jack and Mr. Whitefeather. I told them about the video.

"Wait, she had what?" Dalton asked.

"It was thermal imaging. High tech."

He pondered this. "Okay, go on."

I told them about Don and Carl, the rude cowboys I'd encountered in the hills, then at the Roadhouse.

All the while they nodded, listening.

Then I told them about the stock show, how Dennis had pinned Katy and I'd cold-cocked him.

Dalton grinned.

And how Raina had seen it, how I'd followed her.

"Wait, you actually caught her breaking and entering?"

"Yeah, but it wasn't worth blowing my cover to arrest her."

"I understand, but it speaks to who this woman is."

"I know. There's more." I told him about the land dispute story she was investigating and our agreement, how I'd faced off with Emmett at the diner. "Then you got here," I said to Tom, "and we headed up to talk to Hector."

He nodded. "That didn't get us anywhere."

"A stiff back for you and a dead chicken on my car. I'm pissing someone off with my questions." I told them about my conversation with Casey. "Then I went to talk with the governor."

Mike stood up. "No wonder he didn't cave. You've got nothing." He looked to Tom, then Dalton. "We have no case. There's nothing here but her wishful thinking."

"Hey," Tom said. "Don't be such a dick."

"Don't look at me. I'm not one of the three blind mice here.

She said it herself, Wade had solid evidence it's wolves, and the video seals the deal. What are we even still doing here?"

"Let's take a deep breath," Dalton said. "Maybe Wade is innocent. But something else might be going on. That Raina's involvement doesn't add up for me."

"Why? She's a journalist. They're all shady."

"That aside, if Poppy thinks something else is going on, I think we owe it to her to look into it."

Mike smirked. "Of course you do, since you're sleeping with her."

Dalton stepped toward Mike and, like a flash, Tom was between them. "All right, all right. Let's all take a step back. Take a breath." He faced Mike. "That was uncalled for, man. Sit down."

Mike glared at him.

"Sit down!"

He shrugged and plopped down in the chair.

"We're a team and we're going to act like one. We've got less than two days." He faced Dalton. "What do *you* think we should do?"

Dalton didn't say anything at first. He looked at Mike, then Tom, then me. "I think Poppy was on the right track. We just ratchet it up a notch. Tom, keep doing what you were doing, but really kick the bushes. Mike, those cowboys, Bobby and Bart, get in their faces, see what you can shake out."

He threw his hands in the air. "Oh, you can't be serious?"

Tom was nodding. "Okay. That's what we'll do." He seemed to realize something I didn't. "C'mon, Mike. Let's get back to work."

"No."

Tom spun on him. "It's less than two days. And you're going to give it to her. You got it? Or so help me, if you ever need us at your backs, we'll leave you flapping in the wind. Am I clear?"

Mike got up from the chair and followed Tom out the door,

seething.

I slumped onto the bed. "It doesn't matter. It's over. There's nothing new that's going to come to light. I've been here for almost two weeks and I have nothing. Not one suspect, not one bit of evidence. No one is doing anything wrong. At least the way the government sees it."

Dalton sat down next to me. "But your gut is telling you something's going on. Right?"

I nodded.

"My bet is on that Raina woman. She knows something. And unlike Casey, she has different motivation for keeping it to herself. We need to figure out what it is."

"I doubt she knows anything relevant. She's investigating a land dispute."

"Is she?"

I thought about the implication. "Well, I doubt she knows anything about the wolf issue."

"I think she does. And, if I were a betting man, I'd put my money on that she's no journalist either."

"Feels like a long shot bet. What made you come to that conclusion?"

"I didn't."

"I thought you just said—"

"You did. I can tell by the way you've presented her. You suspect something there. She's the whole reason you won't give up."

I thought about it for a moment. It was true.

"I guess I'll go talk to her again."

"What have you got to lose?"

I was exhausted, but the clock was ticking. Raina was likely to be at the Roadhouse, so I headed that way.

The night was dark with a thin fog and the beams of my headlights barely cut through to see the road as I drove.

When I pulled into the parking lot, I could see right away that Raina's motorhome wasn't here, but I parked anyway and headed in. She might have caught a ride with Emmett.

The place was nearly deserted. Seemed the county was still nursing the collective hangover. Casey wasn't here either. I turned and headed right back out. I'd have to drive all the way to Julie's farm, to the pull out, to talk to Raina. Another fifteen miles.

As I got back into the car, I had a strange feeling, like I was being watched. The hair on the back of my neck stood up. I scanned the parking lot. Nothing. *You're over-tired, McVie.*

With a turn of the key, I fired up the engine, slid the gear shifter to drive, and rolled out of the lot and down the road. In moments, headlights came up behind me, out of nowhere, and passed me on the left. The truck swerved into the lane in front of me, then slammed on the brakes.

What the hell?

As I hit my brakes, I glanced in the rearview mirror. Another set of headlights was right on my tail, closing in. *Bam!* The vehicle behind me rammed my bumper.

I let my foot off the brake and the truck in front of me hit his again. The bright red lights flashed in my eyes as I rammed him from behind.

Crap! I slowed to a stop and quickly memorized the license plate, but I wanted to know who it was right now. The passenger door was flung open and someone wearing a mask rushed toward my car with something in his hands. It was raised in the air and a bucket full of blood splashed against my windshield.

"Hey!" I yelled, shoving my door open. I was on my feet. "What the hell?"

From behind, I heard footsteps, then the liquid hit my back. Warm and sticky, soaking my shirt. Someone appeared beside me. I turned and a full bucket splashed in my face.

"Go home, wolf lover. You don't belong here."

My throat constricted and I felt bile bubble up at the back of my throat. I spun on the speaker, blood dripping from my hair into my eyes. "You son-of-a-bitch!"

He was running back to his truck. The driver's side door slammed, the truck rammed into gear, and he peeled out. The truck in front of me did the same, his wheels spinning, throwing gravel at me.

"That all you've got? A bucket of blood? You cowards," I shouted at their taillights as they disappeared in the night.

Dammit!

Blood soaked my shirt, my pants, my hair. My muscles clenched with disgust.

I took a deep breath, then, carefully, so I didn't drip blood on the cloth seats, reached into the car for my phone and called the local police. I needed an official report to deal with the damage to my rental car. And it's what my cover would do.

Then I started to pull up another number. But I hesitated. I could handle this by myself. I didn't need him. But I was dripping in blood. Nasty, sticky blood. The bile stirred in my stomach again, threatening to erupt. I made the call.

Dalton answered. "Everything all right?"

"It will be, as soon as you get here."

CHAPTER 18

Dalton arrived with towels and the motel ice bucket filled with water. "The things you get yourself into," he said, shaking his head, trying to lighten the mood by teasing me.

"Kinda reminds you of that time in Mexico, huh?" I said, wiping blood from my face with a wet towel.

"Yeah, something like that. What am I going to do with you?"

"I don't know. But what happens in Mexico, stays in Mexico. Same with Idaho."

"Right."

A police car pulled up behind my car, the headlights making me squint. The officer got out of the vehicle and approached, hands on his hips, eyeing my bloody windshield. Then his eyes landed on me. He smirked. "What brought this on? You been shooting your mouth off or something?"

Wow. So much for victim's rights. Or any kind of neutral bias. *Asshole.* I was dripping in blood. I wasn't in the mood. "Yeah, this is all my fault. I've been asking for it," I said, my words laced with angry sarcasm.

"You know what," Dalton said, stepping between me and the officer. "She's a little shaken up. If you don't mind, I'd be happy to stay, answer questions, whatever, but can we let the lady go get a shower right away?"

"Did you witness what happened?"

"No, I wasn't here, but," he looked at me, deciding something, "neither did she really. A couple of trucks pushed her off the road. One in front, one behind. Then guys in masks jumped out and dumped the blood on her. She has no idea who they were and she didn't get the license plates. So, that's it."

The officer shifted his weight to his other foot. "That's it, huh? How do I know it wasn't provoked?"

Dalton's jaw tensed. Ever so slightly. "Provoked? You're kidding, right?"

"Not at all," the man said, all smug. He crossed his arms in front of his chest. "I've seen this before. And usually,"—he looked me in the eyes—"it's deserved."

My mouth dropped open. Was this guy serious?

"I think we'll head down to the station, see if we can't get to the bottom of this there."

"What!" *No way.*

"Are you sure that's necessary?" Dalton said. His hands were on his hips now. He wasn't happy, but as usual, he was keeping his cool.

The thought of sitting at a local police station being questioned by this jerk while soaked to the bone in blood made me want to strangle him.

The officer held out his hand, gestured for me to c'mon as he turned toward his cruiser.

I looked at Dalton. No way was I going with that man.

"C'mon. You're coming with me," he said and took a few more steps toward the car.

Unbelievable.

Dalton gave me a reassuring nod and followed the officer. When he turned, Dalton approached, taking something from his pocket. The two spoke for a moment. Then the officer glared at me, but turned, got back in his patrol car, and pulled away.

"What'd you say to him?" I asked when Dalton came back.

"Doesn't matter," he said.

"But he was determined to be an ass. You must've said something—wait, you didn't?"

"Did you want to spend the next three hours down at the station?" His eyebrows shot up. "Like that?"

"But you've blown your cover. You never blow your cover. Ever."

"Eh, I was bored. I've played the Texas billionaire before and the creepy boyfriend thing—"

"Dalton!"

"Forget it. We've got less than forty-eight hours anyway. I wasn't going to get anywhere with Casey in that time."

"But what did you tell him? Because you realize, whatever it was, the whole town will know within hours."

"Does it matter?"

"Yeah it matters."

"C'mon, let's go get you cleaned up."

"Dalton, what did you tell him?"

He huffed. "Fine. I showed him my badge, told him you were a person of interest in an eco-terrorism plot, and that I was undercover, that it took me months to get close, he was going to blow it for me, because we were supposed to have sex for the first time tonight."

I stared at him. "You did not."

A grin formed at the corner of his mouth. "I flashed my badge, asked him to let it go, as a courtesy, and not mention I was here."

"But he will."

He shrugged.

"Dalton!"

"Do you think I was going to let you go sit at the station, like that, and be interrogated by that asshole for hours?"

"If that's what it took to make sure—"

"No way. You said it yourself, Casey's not involved and if he wouldn't tell you anything, he sure as hell wasn't going to give up any information to me. My role was pointless. So, I'm outed as a fed. So what? If we need to, we'll work it to our advantage."

"But you—"

"No buts. Now get in the car. Let's get you cleaned up." He grinned at me. "You're a mess."

Raina's van was parked at the Johnson ranch this morning. I couldn't approach her there, not for the conversation I wanted to have. I had to wait and get to her when she was alone.

Greg had confirmed the truck from last night was a Split Fork ranch vehicle. I'd figured it was probably Carl and Don, the same jerks who'd harassed me before. But they worked at the Johnson farm.

Luckily, the damage to the car had been minimal; it was still drivable. Dalton's hotel shower might never be the same though. It took me hours to feel clean again. Then he didn't want me to head back to Gladys's place alone. I didn't want to either.

At dawn, we'd headed north again, in our separate cars, and took turns driving by the farm, watching for Raina to leave. The problem was, she might be there all day or even overnight.

I'd drive by, then pull over and pace, waiting to get Dalton's signal. Then I'd head back the other way, pull over and pace. This was getting me nowhere. The clock tick-tocked in my head. It might as well have been the sound of those wolves, crying for my help.

In the late morning, Dalton called. "Let's take a break and get lunch."

"What if she leaves?"

"If she does, it will probably be to get lunch. C'mon, you've got to eat."

We met at the diner. It was a quiet weekday and we arrived a little before the usual lunch hour. We had our pick of the booths. Dalton let me take the side where I could watch the door.

Diane took our orders, her eyes lingering on Dalton a little too long. Had she already heard about last night? Did everyone in town already know he was a federal agent? It didn't matter, like he said. By this time tomorrow, the wolves would be shot and I'd call Hyland and tell her I'd failed to find any wrong doing. And that would be that.

When my food arrived, I stared at it.

"You need to eat," Dalton said.

"Why blood do you think?"

He shrugged. "I don't know. Maybe they'd slaughtered some cows yesterday and someone got the bright idea. Who knows. Try not to think about it."

"Were they saying their blood is on me? The wolves' blood? That this is my fault?"

"Don't do this to yourself. None of this is your fault."

I looked up. "No. I know. I just wonder if…"

He shook his head. "You wonder what?"

"If this is how my dad felt."

Dalton reached across the table, took my hand in his, and squeezed.

The door swung open and Casey walked in. His eyes met mine, then he saw Dalton, holding my hand. He went straight to a bar stool at the counter without saying a word, and sat facing the kitchen.

"I'll be right back," I said and got up and sat down on the stool next to Casey. "Hey there."

He looked over his shoulder at Dalton before acknowledging me. "Hey there."

I figured he'd already heard about Dalton, which means he'd already heard about last night. He probably already heard from Gladys, too.

In a quiet voice, he said, "So, you leaving town soon?"

"Do you know about last night? What happened to me?"

He stared for a moment, then looked away. It was a quick

moment, but long enough for me to know.

"What is it about this place?" I said, not hiding my frustration.

He turned back to me with a little shrug. "It's home." He nodded toward Dalton. "So, he's your boyfriend?"

I was already off the stool. "Yeah. The love of my life."

I scarfed down my lunch and we headed back out to find Raina. Her van was still at the ranch. What was she doing there, anyway?

We took up the same routine. I'd drive by, then pull over and pace, waiting to get Dalton's signal. Then I'd head back the other way, pull over and pace.

Just before dark, a helicopter arrived, landing in the Johnson field. They'd be heading out into the mountains, armed to kill, first thing in the morning.

Around eleven o'clock, when I thought my nerves couldn't take another minute, Dalton called, said she'd left the ranch, headed south, and turned on the side road, probably to park in her spot at the edge of Julie's farm for the night.

Hallelujah! "I'll be right there," I told him. "Make sure she doesn't leave again."

I zoomed down the road, breaking the sound barrier in my rental.

As I turned in and parked, she opened the door to greet me. "Hey Poppy, how'd it go with Casey?"

"Can we talk inside?"

"Sure," she said, pushing the door open by way of invitation. "I'll put on some tea."

I followed her into the motorhome. As she filled the teakettle, I looked around, really seeing it again for the first time. The wood cabinets, the plush seats, the little stainless appliances. This was a top-of-the-line rig, and no doubt, had the price tag to go with it. Not likely something an unknown journalist could afford. My first instinct had been right on.

She sat down at the table. "Well, how was your date?"

"It went well. I'll tell you all about it, if you tell me everything you know." I reached into my pocket.

"I told you—"

I dropped my badge on her table.

She let out a puff of air. Her eyes slowly met mine. "You're good. Really good. I had no idea."

"Thanks." I sat down across from her. "But I don't need compliments. I need to know everything you know."

"Are you arresting me?"

I shook my head. "No. Should I?"

She stared, gave a subtle shake of her head.

"I have a feeling you have information I need. I'm hoping you'll cooperate."

"Information about what, exactly?"

"Just start from the beginning. You're not Julie's aunt, I'm sure of that. And you're willing to commit crimes to do… whatever it is you're doing."

"Why didn't you arrest me when you caught me in Emmett's house?"

"I have discretion in those matters. It didn't serve my investigation to out myself, at the time."

She leaned back, her shoulders slumped. "Well, what do you want to know?"

"You're not really a journalist."

"No. But I love the irony that you aren't either."

"Are you really investigating a land dispute?"

She thought for a moment before she answered. "Sort of."

"Am I going to have to keep asking questions to drag it all out of you?"

Her eyes held mine. This woman was smart. She was trying to figure out what she'd get out of this encounter. Finally, she started talking. "You're right. I'm not a journalist, though it's a good cover. And I'm not a criminal. Though I'm not going to lie, I will do whatever it takes to do my job. You see, the group I work for, they have a vested interest in Julie's farm project."

"What kind of interest?"

"They gave her the loan. Only, she doesn't know that. They're silent investors. Really silent."

"Go on."

"This group, they don't just give loans, then walk away. They are very particular about who they support. They keep a close eye on things, make sure the women they fund have everything they need to succeed. If anything happens to jeopardize that, they send me in to assess the situation."

"So, you're some kind of assessor? An assessor that does whatever it takes, even if it's outside the law?"

She nodded with confidence. "Yeah, that about sums it up."

"But you were already here, *before* the wolves attacked the chickens. That's why you have the video. You already suspected something else was jeopardizing the farm project."

The teakettle whistled. She got up, poured hot water into our cups, handed one to me, then carried hers over and sat back down. "Yes. Mr. Johnson has been on Julie to sell since the day her grandmother died."

"But you said she couldn't sell, that the land was in a trust."

"It is. He didn't know that at first. He does now. But that doesn't change the fact that he wants access to her land. He's been harassing her, doing everything he can to make her life miserable, and to make sure she fails. He wants nothing more than for her to have to move back to the city and abandon everything." She crossed her arms. "I swear, at this point, he's doing it out of spite. The threats keep getting dirtier."

"Okay, so you showed up to do what? How'd you plan to make him stop?"

"I told you, I came to assess the situation. But yes, also to see if there was something I could do to make him stop. I was working on a plan for just that. Right now, he thinks, as her aunt, that I have some influence to persuade her."

"So, that's a long term con. Meanwhile, you've set up security measures, the video cameras, hoping to catch him doing something, anything?"

"Typical protocol, yeah."

"I bet he was thrilled about the wolf incident then. A tragic blow he had no hand in."

"Yeah." She took a sip of her tea. Her eyes focused on me, but her mind was deep in thought somewhere else. "So, if you don't mind me saying, you haven't answered my question. What are you investigating exactly? Must be some kind of serious criminal activity, or they'd send someone in a shirt and tie, not an undercover agent."

Interesting moment to switch gears. I'd play along. "With all the wolf depredation, we suspected the local Wildlife Services agent of defrauding the government by conspiring with the ranchers to make claims for reimbursement. As far as I can tell, he's clean. In fact, your video proves it was wolves. At least at Julie's farm."

She sat up straight, leaned forward. "Let me make sure I understand. You're saying that, if it wasn't really wolves, and someone knew that, but made a claim anyway, they'd be committing a felony?"

"Possibly. It's definitely a crime. The specific crime and punishment depends on the circumstances, dollar amounts, intent, etcetera."

That mind was at it again, thinking, contemplating. "If I had information, information that could implicate someone, could you get a search warrant?"

Now we were getting somewhere. "It depends what you mean by information. I would need probable cause." Regardless of what she told me, there was no way I could get a warrant in time to save the wolves. The helicopter was lifting off first thing in the morning. "Tell me what you know."

"I know you want to stop that wolf hunt tomorrow." She stared. "So, can you get a search warrant right now?"

I shook my head. "No. I don't have those kinds of connections here."

She got up, paced to the sink, set her cup down, thought a moment, staring out the window, then came back and sat down. "Okay, this could work. Not what I'd planned, but it could work. Hear me out. So, you saw me poking around, very suspiciously the other night in Mr. Johnson's house. Right?"

I nodded. Where was she going with this?

"So, when you came by to question me about it tonight, and you saw me slip away in the dark, you thought you should follow me, right?"

"Okay. Where am I following you to?"

"If a suspect were to trespass on someone else's private property, you could follow, legally, right?"

"In this scenario, you're the suspect?"

"Exactly."

Okay, this was an interesting approach. "Well, there is exception for exigent circumstances. There's a hot pursuit clause. Service officers may pursue a suspect onto private premises if they have probable cause to arrest the suspect."

"If you knew I'd committed a crime, or you were suspicious enough to try to catch me in the act of a crime. That could work."

"Are you planning to commit a crime?"

"No. But you might be suspecting me, right? Maybe something I said, I don't know, work with me here. I guess you could even out me for breaking and entering before."

"Okay. I could see that scenario."

"And if it so happened, during said hot pursuit, that you came across some other, unexpected evidence, that you could use…"

Omigod, spit it out! "What are you saying? Do you have knowledge of this evidence?"

"I have a hunch."

"A hunch?"

"A strong hunch. Okay, good reason to believe."

Ugh. I wanted to throttle her. *Is this what it feels like for Dalton when I tell him about my hunches?*

"I didn't know what to do with the information until now. But if you can…" She paused as though she needed a moment to decide whether to plunge forward. "I'd have to disappear afterwards, of course. I got no patience for being questioned at police stations. I'll leave that for you to sort out."

"What information?" I said.

"You see, the video Julie showed you, that was a short clip of the longer video."

"What else was on the video? Show me."

"Doesn't matter. The video proves nothing, in and of itself."

I stared. This woman made me want to tear my hair out.

"But now, it all makes sense."

"No, it doesn't. You're not making any sense. Maybe I should just cuff you and drag you down to the station."

She grinned. She knew I wasn't serious. "It will. If I'm right. It will all make sense. And I'm sure I'm right." She rose from the seat, got a coat from the tiny closet, grabbed a flashlight, and headed for the door. "I'm gonna go for that walk. You should follow me."

This is nuts.

"Bring your badge."

CHAPTER 19

The moon only hinted at rising in the eastern sky. As I followed her out of the motorhome, into the blackness, I needed a moment for my eyes to adjust. And my brain. I didn't like someone else calling the shots, withholding information. But I had a feeling it was play along, or forget it. And this might be my only chance.

This was crazy. She could have been leading me to the deep woods, into a trap. But I knew she wasn't. She cared about Julie. Her story made perfect sense. And she didn't have much time to make it all up. The odds were good that it was true. Still, why didn't she tell me where we were heading, and what we'd find? Maybe she wasn't sure. Maybe she wanted me to have plausible deniability. Was that even relevant here? *Plausible deniability?*

Regardless, I'd already made the decision.

My dad always said to follow my gut. *Is that what he had done? Is that what got him killed?*

We crept through the wet meadow, crossing Julie's farm in the dark, moving as quickly as we could. Finally, we were on the Johnson property, where I'd figured we'd end up. My pants were soaked through and my toes squished inside my shoes.

"This way," Raina said.

She stayed to the eastern side of the property, along the river bank, as far from the house and detection as possible.

"Where are you taking me?" I whispered.

"Patience," she said, like some sort of sensei. At least she didn't call me grasshopper.

Soon, we were in the woods and it was as though a shade had been pulled over a window. Raina flicked on the flashlight. It glowed red. Smart. Red doesn't affect night vision and it's not bright enough to be seen from a distance.

She shined it ahead of us, lighting the way.

Progress was slow, but every step took us closer to our destination, wherever that was. It was well past midnight by now.

"You know, I'm putting a lot of trust in you here," I said.

"Yes. Just remember what I said."

"Which part? That this is all based on a hunch?"

"That you followed me. I want to be sure anything you find is admissible. Because if this goes the way I plan, my job will be done here."

I came to a halt. "I'm not sure—"

She swung around. "Promise me you'll prosecute, to the fullest extent of the law. End this thing for Julie. She deserves a fair shot."

"Okay." I had no idea what I'd be arresting anyone for, but okay. "I'll do everything I can. If there's criminal activity. But, unfortunately, just because Mr. Johnson has been an ass doesn't mean—"

"Not him. Denny."

"Oh." Denny. The creep who'd pinned Katy, the one I'd given a black eye. Now I wasn't sure this was such a good idea.

"Emmett is angry about the land, but I'm sure it's Denny who's taken matters into his own hands. He's the violent one."

"Now there is something I can corroborate. But you think whatever he's been up to is certifiable criminal behavior?"

"Believe me, if it's what I suspect...I have a feeling you're good at connecting dots. It will all make sense. Just follow me."

We moved through the forest, slowly, but on a determined path.

The deeper we got into the Johnson property, the more cautiously she proceeded. Finally, we arrived near a structure, tucked deep in the woods. The canopy above was so thick, this building would never be seen from an aerial view. I wondered if that was purposeful.

"What is it?" I asked.

"You need to see for yourself," she said, motioning for me to follow.

I walked behind her, placing my feet in her footsteps. When we got closer, I could see a six-foot chain link fence on the north side of the structure.

"Is this a dog kennel?" I whispered. "I thought that huge barn up by the house was his kennel."

"It is."

We crept closer.

There was movement inside. Sounds of animals. Then the barking started.

Raina came to a halt. "We need to be quick. Get a look inside and take off."

She started forward and a spotlight flicked on, then another, then another. We both froze. The lights must have been triggered by a motion detector. She turned to me, a look of indecision on her face.

"You need to get a look."

From inside the kennel, we heard the clank of gate latches.

Our eyes met. *What the hell?*

In seconds, a pack of snarling dogs came through the barn doors, charging at us, jaws snapping.

"Holy shit! Run!"

The barking and snarling morphed into a singular roar behind me as I sprinted double-time into the woods, branches and leaves whipping at my face. We didn't have a chance. Not against a pack of hungry dogs. There was no way we could outrun them. We had seconds before they'd be on us.

"Go! Go! Go!" Raina yelled beside me.

"Get up a tree!" My legs burned and my heartbeat thumped in my ears as I tore through a patch of ferns in a dead sprint. "It's our only chance."

By the light of the spotlights, I saw a good tree ahead, with low branches. I went right at it, leaped, grabbed the first branch, and swung myself up. Once I had purchase, I turned. "Give me your hand."

Raina was there, reaching for me. I grabbed her wrist. Her hand latched onto my wrist and I pulled with all my might. Up she came, just as the dogs reached the base of the tree, yipping and yowling as they spun, frustrated.

"Climb higher." I reached for the next branch and pulled myself up. Raina followed. I straddled the branch, huffing and heaving.

"That's what—" Raina wheezed, trying to catch her breath.

The six dogs barking and twisting in a frenzy below us were huge, easily one hundred and fifty pounds each. And they had a distinct look. Pointed ears. Thick coat.

Undeniable. They were hybrids. Wolf-dogs.

Denny must have been secretly breeding wild wolves with domestic dogs.

"Holy crap!" she said. "I didn't expect someone to be in there."

"Yeah, well…"

"That's illegal, right?"

"Yes." So was siccing them on a federal agent. "Without a permit, for sure. States have different laws, but yes."

"Okay. Now what?"

"Now what? This was *your* plan."

"Plan? I told you it was a hunch. I didn't know he'd set them loose."

Well, shit. Did he actually see us? Or had he set them loose to chase whatever had set off the motion detectors? Would he call them off? Then what?

The dogs settled into huffs and whines. Two lay down at the base of the tree. The whole ridiculous situation reminded me of Honey Bear, a black bear I'd saved from a couple of poachers in Michigan. They'd set loose a pack of hound dogs that chased her down. She'd taken refuge in a tree only to be darted with a tranquilizer. They'd planned to sell her to a bear bile farm. But they hadn't counted on me hiding in the bushes. Those jerks were in a federal penitentiary, where they belonged.

If my memory served me, their dogs would've waited at the bottom of that tree for days if they needed to. I was pretty sure these dogs would too.

I pulled my phone from my pocket, clicked it on to read the display. "No service."

"Me neither. Maybe they'll get bored and give up and go home," she said.

"I don't think that's going to happen."

"What's our plan, then? Hang around and wait?" She huffed. "No pun intended."

"Hey, I'm winging it here."

One of the dogs, the alpha I bet, stood tall, staring at me, his gaze a primal warning.

"I don't see any other choice. If we drop down out of this tree, they'll rip us to shreds."

"Maybe I should've listened to my mom," Raina said. "Be a tax accountant. Job security. Nothing more sure than death and taxes."

"Yeah, I can't picture you doing taxes."

"Me neither. Too much screen time."

We both laughed, that nervous laugh that bubbles out when your nerves are on fire.

Crap. "You didn't bring a slab of steak in your coat pocket, did you?"

"No," she smirked. "I usually don't leave home without one, but…"

"Well, there is some good news."

"Yeah? What's that?"

"I was right. There's no rash of wolf depredation. He used these wolf-dogs to kill Julie's chickens, didn't he? To try to drive her out of her business. But he had to set the stage, so it didn't seem too out of the ordinary. He used them to systematically kill livestock in the area. All the reimbursements the Johnson ranch received was a bonus, and any of the other ranches around in this tight-knit community. Not to mention getting Jack Wade to get rid of the real wolves at the same time."

"Sounds a little complicated for the Denny I know," Raina said. "Maybe Emmett really was the brain behind it."

"But how did you even suspect it was wolf-dogs? I mean, it makes perfect sense now, but, I admit, it never crossed my mind."

"The video. There was a shadow of a man, off to the edge of the frame. I couldn't explain his presence. And no matter what reason he might have had for being there, I figured there was no way a pack of wolves would enter that barn with a human right there, unless they were together. That, and Julie was convinced she hadn't left the door open.

"I admit, I still thought it was wolves though, until you came along. It made me go back and rethink it. That and finding out that Denny breeds dogs. A quick internet search and I found out that dogs and wolves share DNA. So, if Jack had taken samples, he'd still think it was wild wolves."

I looked down at the hybrid canines. The one was still staring at me, his lips pulled back to show his teeth, drool hanging from his mouth. "They look wild. Worse than wild. If they're under Denny's command."

The alpha was still staring, unflinching. He wasn't going anywhere.

This is a fine kettle of fish. What the hell do we do?

The low rumble of an engine starting up echoed inside the barn. The throttle was revved up, then, a few moments later, a four-wheeler appeared, its headlight flashing in our eyes as it bumped and joggled over the terrain.

The ATV rolled to a stop about twenty yards from the tree. Denny killed the engine and sat on the machine, staring up at us, a wicked laugh gurgling from his mouth. "Well, well, well. What do we have here?"

"Would you please call off your dogs?" I said.

"Now why would I wanna do that?"

He swung his leg over the seat and was on his feet, sauntering toward us, rays of the headlight glinting off that huge belt buckle.

"You know what we do to trespassers here in Idaho?" From behind his back, he brought out a handgun and pointed it right at me. "We shoot, shovel, and shut up."

CHAPTER 20

"You don't want to do that," I said, trying not to sound as frantic as I was feeling. "We called for help. They'll be here any minute."

He laughed, that same wicked laugh. "I don't believe you. There's no service out here." He raised the gun to aim.

"I thought so, too. But, as luck would have it, I guess I'm high enough in this tree because I got one bar."

He hesitated. *Good.*

Keep talking. Keep him thinking, doubting. "I had to text, of course. But it went through."

He squinted his eyes. Shoot, shovel, and shut up was one thing. Getting twenty years to life for murder was another.

"Listen, this is all a misunderstanding anyway." *Think. A plausible reason to be out here in the middle of the night.* "Sannyu, Katy's dog, took off, didn't come home. We've been out trying to find him, and well, when it got dark, we kinda got turned around."

"Right. And I'm a monkey's uncle."

What does that even mean?

"It's true," Raina said, her tone one of a scolding mother. "Now call off your dogs, Denny. This is ridiculous. I'm getting a damn splinter."

The pistol came up again. He leveled the sights on me, a new confidence in his eyes. "Throw me your phone."

"What? No." *Crap.*

"Throw it down to me, right now, or I'll shoot. I swear to God."

"No you won't." I hoped. And if he did... He was at least fifteen yards away. Accuracy with a handgun dropped off considerably past ten feet. And I was in a raised position. Accuracy dropped more when shooting upward.

Who am I kidding? Looking down the barrel of a pistol held by a psychopath was scary as hell, no matter how much training you've had. Especially one who'd I'd humiliated and gave a black eye. My heart was hammering in my chest and my hands were shaking. We were sitting ducks.

The good news was, he hadn't shot yet. I focused on that.

"I will, you bitch. Now throw it down."

"Nope. You tie up your dogs and I'll bring it down. Then you can decide if you want to shoot me, though I'm telling you right now, our friends are on the way. Your shoot-shovel-and-shut-up plan isn't going to fly. "

"That so? Phhht." He turned and went back to his four-wheeler. Attached to the handlebars was a two-way radio. He held it to his mouth and pushed the button. "Carl, get out here and get the dogs."

The smug son of a bitch stood with his arms crossed, a grin on his face, staring up at us in the tree as we waited. Finally, another four-wheeler arrived. Carl got off. He looked up at me and smirked. "It's you, huh? I bet the dogs could smell you a mile away."

Jerk. I'd scrubbed and scrubbed, but he was probably right. These hounds could probably still smell the cow's blood on me.

Denny shouted orders at him over the sound of the engine. "Take these dogs, and the other four, up in the hills and shoot 'em. I don't want 'em to be found. Got it?"

"Got it, boss."

I swallowed hard. How could he be so cruel? But I knew

the answer. They were the evidence of his crimes. He'd get rid of them, to be sure, in case he couldn't get rid of us, the witnesses. It would be our word against his, and we were the trespassers. Maybe he wasn't so stupid after all.

Carl snapped leashes to the collars on the wolf dogs, one at a time, and got them tied to the back of his four-wheeler. But I couldn't let him go. I couldn't let him kill these animals.

"Hold on! Stop right there," I said, starting down the branches. Raina descended right with me. "I'll give you the phone." I dropped to the ground and rushed toward Denny, holding it out in front of me. "Here's the phone. See?"

His arm stiffened and raised, the gun now aimed at my chest.

I tossed the phone in the air, right at his face.

He jerked to the side, an involuntary reaction to avoid getting hit by it. His gun arm dropped and I was on him. I plowed into him like a WWE wrestler, knocking him to the ground. His left arm came up, but I blocked, pinning it with my elbow. He tried to roll. I rolled with him, bringing my left elbow around, and rammed it into his cheek.

He tried to buck me off. I flexed my leg, bringing my knee upward with a jerk into his groin. He groaned, his body clamping into a fetal position.

The dogs went nuts, barking their heads off.

Carl pounced, low from the side, slamming me onto my back.

"Not so fast, cupcake," Raina said.

She stood over us, Denny's pistol in her hands. "Now get your hands up, or I shoot."

Carl retreated like a beaten mutt.

Denny lay on his side, both hands cupping his crotch. "You bitch!"

I got up, brushed my hands on my pants, and turned to Raina. "Thanks for the backup."

"No problem."

"Mind if I take the firearm?"

"Sure, no problem." She carefully handed it to me, keeping it pointed at the men.

I checked the chamber, made sure it was actually loaded, then held it aimed at Denny. "Maybe you could check for some rope? We need to tie these guys up."

She lifted the seat of Denny's ATV and found a fat roll of duct tape. "This do?"

"Sure."

In minutes, she had them hogtied, lying on their bellies, hands and feet bound together. They looked like they'd been strung up to hang from a spit.

I bent down, examined the bindings. "That can't possibly be comfortable."

"Do we care?" Raina asked.

"Nope."

"What now?"

I stepped away from the men, gesturing for her to follow. "I guess it's time for your disappearing act. I appreciate this, I really do."

She nodded. "Give me one hour. I'll be gone. But do me a favor?"

"Anything."

"Tell Julie and Katy that I said goodbye."

"I promise."

"And don't let that son of bitch get anything less than the maximum."

"That too. And I'll need that video. The full version."

She nodded. "My pleasure. I'll put it in her mailbox."

"I hate to see you go. We make a good team."

"Well, maybe our paths will cross again. Until then, keep up the fight for what's right."

I smiled. That's exactly what I was trying to do.

We walked back toward the men. "Take the four-wheeler," I said. "Oh, let me see your phone." She handed it to me. I typed in Dalton's number and handed it back to her. "When you get out in the meadow, where you have service, give that number a call."

Denny groaned.

"Tell him where I am, that I need his help. You don't need to worry about, you know." She knew I meant her own involvement, but I didn't want to give that away to Denny. "Give the details and send him."

"Will do," she said, and straddled the machine, fired it up, and drove away.

As soon as the roar of the engine was gone, I turned to the men. "By the way, boys, you're under arrest. You have the right to remain silent. Unless you want to confess." I focused on Denny. "It was you, wasn't it? You used these dogs to kill Julie's chickens."

"Screw you."

"Nah, you're right. You really should keep your mouth shut. You are in a lot of trouble." I leaned over him. "See, you've messed with the government. And if I have my way, you're going to spend some time inside a prison cell."

He kept his head down, didn't respond.

"Though I imagine the other ranchers around here won't be too thrilled when they find out it was you who's been killing their livestock." I felt the blood on me again. "Local justice seems to be swift and harsh around here. Maybe I should just let them take care of it."

Before long, a car appeared in the woods, heading this way. Dalton pulled up in his rental car. He'd driven right past the main house, across the property, and down the two-track that led to this hidden dog kennel.

He left the headlights on as he got out of the car, though the sun had already come up. "What's going on here?"

"Got me a haul," I said. For some reason I found that amusing.

He examined the work Raina had done with the duct tape.

"How am I supposed to get them in the car?"

"I don't know and I don't care."

In the distance, an engine roared to life. Then the distinctive whir of propeller blades.

My eyes snapped to Dalton's. "It's eight o'clock already?"

He looked at his watch. "No. Six ten."

Dammit!

I ran to the car, got in the driver's side, threw the gear shifter into reverse, spun the car around, slammed it into drive, and floored the gas pedal.

CHAPTER 21

I raced down the wooded two-track, and as I broke from the trees, into the open field, the helicopter lifted off the ground. I punched down the accelerator pedal. But I was too late.

I slammed on the brakes and jumped out of the car, waving my arms in the air, running to try to get in their view. But the helicopter was directly overhead. They couldn't see me. It rose higher and disappeared over the trees.

Dammit!

Call him. That's what I needed to do. Surely he had a cell phone with him. But I didn't have his number.

As the noise of the helicopter faded, I heard a low voice, chanting.

I spun around, toward the sound. Mr. Whitefeather stood in the field where the helicopter had lifted off. He was dressed in traditional clothing, all fringe and beads. His mournful chant filled the silence that was left.

I ran toward him. "Mr. Whitefeather! Mr. Whitefeather! We need to call them off."

He opened his eyes. An expression of disappointment crossed his face. I'd interrupted something sacred. But it had to be done.

"It wasn't the wolves. I have proof."

When I reached him, he looked at me with the calm wisdom of his age. "What are you saying?"

I held out my badge. "I'm a federal agent. I've been undercover. And I just arrested a man for falsely accusing the wolves for his own killing spree. I can explain all that later. But we need to call Jack and stop him."

He looked at my badge skeptically.

"It's real. I assure you."

"You are from the federal government?"

I nodded.

He reached into his pocket and took out a cell phone. He punched in a number and hit send, listened, then shook his head. "No answer. He probably can't hear the phone ring inside the helicopter."

Dammit! "I have to stop that helicopter."

He thought for a moment. "Air traffic control? But I don't know who has the authority to—"

"I do." I took out my own phone and found the number for the Governor's office. When the line was picked up, I said, "Ted Montgomery, please. Tell him it's an emergency."

"Who shall I say is calling?"

"Special Agent Poppy McVie, representing the President of the United States."

"Yes, ma'am. Please hold."

Two excruciatingly long minutes later, he came on the line. "This better be good."

"I've arrested a man with a pack of wolf-dog hybrids. I have reason to believe he's been using them to kill the livestock."

"Well, I'm not sure how—"

"I need you to call air traffic control to hail Jack Wade in that helicopter and tell him to stand down. Right now."

"I can't just—"

"Right now! Or so help me, I'll make it my personal—"

"All right."

"I'm going to hold on the line while you do it."

"Fine." There was dead air for another four minutes. I paced, staring at Mr. Whitefeather, then to the hill where the helicopter had disappeared. Finally, the governor's assistant returned to the line. "It's done."

Every muscle I'd been holding taut relaxed and I had to sit down in the grass.

Mr. Whitefeather sat down next to me. "You have a been a good friend to He'me."

"I just hope he made the call in time."

"He did. I can feel it. He'me lives on."

Ten minutes later, I heard the distinctive rumble of the propeller blades as the helicopter came over the hill. Mr. Whitefeather and I covered our faces as it descended to the ground, then cut the engines.

The side door popped open and Jack hopped to the ground.

I ran toward him. "Had you found them yet? Did you shoot?"

He shook his head. "Not one shot." He smiled at me, obviously glad.

I stared at the phone in my hand.

"What'd she say?" Dalton asked.

"She's Hyland, how can we ever truly know? It's like she talks in code, I swear."

He smirked. "No kidding."

"Apparently she got a call from the governor, thanking her."

He squeezed my hand. "You didn't want accolades anyway. It was about the wolves for you. Right?"

"Of course. But I'm glad to still have my job."

"Are you?"

I looked into his eyes. Was I? The job had changed. I'd changed. "I don't like politics. I like being in the field, chasing the bad guys, relying on my wits and skills."

"Are you saying you don't want to be on this team anymore?" He asked with no inclination of his own opinion.

"I don't know. Do you?"

"I don't know."

"Hyland said she wants us to head to Louisiana. Details coming."

"Uh-huh."

I shrugged.

We sat next to each other in silence for a moment.

"Tom said something the other night. He said we've got a lot of latitude, and what Hyland doesn't know…"

"He makes a good point."

I nodded.

He fidgeted, then drew in a breath. "Are you mad at me for going to Africa?"

I shook my head. "Nah. But we need to talk about it."

"Yeah."

"I need to go."

"I know."

Dalton, Tom, Jack Wade, and I sat around Julie's table. Mike refused a seat, said he might never sit down again, then shot daggers at me with his eyes. I shrugged. He'd live.

Julie had made another amazing egg dish. This one she called Artichoke, Kale & Ricotta Pie.

Katy cleared the table and was in the kitchen, washing the dishes.

"So, I can't believe it," Julie said, folding her napkin. "It's all over. No more hassle from the Johnsons."

"That's all thanks to Raina," I said.

"I know. I want to thank her, but I have no idea how to contact her. She showed up one day, said she'd take care of things. And I guess she did. Now she's gone. Without a word." She grinned. "I feel like, *who was that masked woman*?"

"A Lone Ranger, that's for sure."

"So, what's going to happen to Denny?" she asked.

"The Director of Internal Services and Consumer Protection at the Department of Agriculture will investigate the allegations of fraud. Essentially, he was lying to the federal government by making the false claims and wasting Mr. Wade's time, and the state government by applying for the compensation for livestock allegedly depredated on the Johnson farm. He's also responsible for the claims of others because he killed their livestock, not wolves. It's a nice long list of crimes.

"The local detective did find strychnine in Denny's barn. He was the one doing that, too. And of course he'll be busted for possession and breeding of the wolf-dogs without a permit. I don't know yet if Mr. Johnson will be convicted as well. We're turning the investigation over to the state. They'll also determine how much Casey knew, though I doubt he was involved at all.

"And there's one more thing. If Katy wants, I'd like to talk to authorities about his aggressive behavior at the dog show. And get her someone she can talk to about her feelings, too."

Julie nodded, her eyes moist. "I can't thank you enough."

"It's my job," I said, not knowing what else to say. "I can't wait to see what you accomplish here at New Hope Farm. I think it's wonderful what you're building for those kids."

Tom spoke up. "I was able to contact a real representative of the non-lethal strategies program to take over and help those I actually did get to sign up."

"That's great," Julie said. She turned back to me. "Where will you go next?"

I shrugged. "Wherever we're needed."

Author's Note

I wasn't sure whether I wanted to tackle the BIG issue of wolves. Wow, the more I researched, the deeper the rabbit hole became. Talk about a political mess...

To be clear, I always do my very best to portray the animal issues accurately and clarify the stuff I've made up for the fiction. This story is set in a fictional town, but based in reality from the many accounts I've read of exactly how outsiders, especially those who support animal rights, are often treated in rural Idaho, Montana, and Wyoming.

There have been countless instances of tourists in Yellowstone getting way too close to the bison. I have a close friend who witnessed a parent attempt to set his child on a bison's back, just as described. It's mind boggling to me.

I hope you enjoyed this story. Thank YOU so much for reading. If you're interested in connecting with me online, I like to share travel stories (like my own trip to Yellowstone) and videos (Have you ever seen a napping sloth? This is exciting stuff!), my wildlife photos, and MORE! Please sign up for my newsletter at www.KimberliBindschatel.com. You'll be the FIRST to know about my new releases, too. (I have a special sign-up gift for you.) Join the adventure.

THANK YOU

Thanks to my good friend, Steve Kamerling, for describing exactly what happens with strychnine and what it would take to save a dog who'd ingested it.

Katy Bertodatto's editing made this story shine. Rachel, as usual, kept me focused on what matters.

I am so thankful for my proof readers—Cathy, Annie, and Cynthia. They went above and beyond, and at the very last minute.

I get to do this because of the loving support of my husband. And he often has great suggestions. The wolf-dog hybrid was his idea. Genius.

As always, thanks to my parents for raising me with a deep love of animals.

Most of all, thank YOU for reading and supporting this indie author. If you feel as strongly as I do about the issues presented in this book and you want to help, PLEASE tell a friend about the story. Help me spread the word. You, too, can make a difference! For the animals!

If you'd like to be the FIRST to know about my new releases, please sign up for my newsletter at www.KimberliBindschatel. com. Plus, I share travel stories and videos, my wildlife photos, and MORE! Join the adventure.

ABOUT THE AUTHOR

Kimberli A. Bindschatel is a thrill seeker, travel adventurer, passionate animal lover, wildlife photographer and award-winning author of the Amazon Best-selling Poppy McVie Mystery series.

When she's not busting bad guys with her pen, she's out in the wilderness getting an adrenaline fix. She has rappelled down a waterfall in Costa Rica, rafted the Grand Canyon, faced down an Alaskan grizzly bear at ten feet (camera in hand), snorkeled with stingrays, and white-water kayaked a Norwegian river. She's always ready for an adventure.

She lives in northern Michigan where she loves to hike in the woods with her rescue dog, Josee, share a bottle of wine with good friends, or sail Lake Michigan with her husband on their boat, *Priorities*. (You gotta have your priorities!)

Kimberli also co-writes the Charity Styles Caribbean Thriller series with Best-selling author, Wayne Stinnett.

She loves sharing her passion for adventure and wildlife with her readers and happily gives away some of her award-winning wildlife photos. Sign up for her newsletter at www.kimberlibindschatel.com and get a free photograph for your desktop.

What will Poppy do next?

OPERATION

BAYOU
JUSTICE

KIMBERLI A. BINDSCHATEL

A black market exporter is getting greedy...
...trading precious animals like currency.
One woman will take him down.

Special Agent Poppy McVie and her partner are undercover, setting a trap for a notorious criminal. But their informant isn't making it easy. He's none too happy about his plea deal and life on a tether.

As they close in on the target, Poppy makes a shocking discovery. A mistake from her past has come back to haunt her. As events spin out of control and the danger escalates, Poppy must risk it all to confront an old nemesis. Can she lure him out of the swamp, or will she wind up as gator bait?